SCROLLS

of

ARCADIA

Part I

DR. MURTAZA H. SYED

I would like to dedicate this book to my father who made me write one page of literature a day when I was young along with all my school homework. Also, to my son, Isa—who was my main motivation behind writing this book—you have always been a guiding light for me in the darkest of times. I hope you know that. My mother and two sisters, Shahla and Tania, may Allah bless you and keep you safe. To all my friends who supported me in my hardest times but most of all to Allah, who was there when no one else was, thank you. Last, to my readers who helped make my dreams come true, I appreciate you all and would like to show you gratitude by saying thank you to you, too, for all your support! God bless!

TABLE OF CONTENTS

PROLOGUE

In front of the Council of Crystals, Jerreria spoke out loudly, "Do you not know the depth of what is going on? All seven heavens are at risk of being overtaken!" He was of average height, close to six feet. He had a slight beard, not too long and black in color. His skin was the color of sand and seemed to have a glitter or shine to it like a beach on a hot day. He wore a dark blue garment that didn't appear ironed, which he liked because he thought it looked good on him when he rode Zulgini.

"Now, now, Jerreria. What evidence do you have to support such paradox claims?" one of the elders asked as the rest fell silent, awaiting an answer.

This made Jerreria uneasy and reluctant to speak the truth. Word had been slowly getting around Arcadia that hidden evils were at work. Evils that wanted nothing more than the demise of the seven heavens and the universe as they knew it.

"Three of the five scrolls are missing and the locations of the last two are unknown. Each scroll contains knowledge of all Arcadia that governs the universe itself. If all five fall into the wrong hands, the cage of eternal fire can be extinguished, and the Evil One Dajjrah will be free. Gateways to all seven heavens will be compromised and everyone's eternal happiness along with them!"

Wizards gasped and snickered among themselves. Some were in shock, and others were frustrated. Jerreria's eyes searched the room for someone who believed him, but he was met with hateful stares. Jerreria was different from other wizards. He was something of a wizard genius; he had the ability to learn and adapt quickly, and he worked well under a great deal of pressure. When he had been sent to the Island of Dragons, Father Dragon had appointed him the most amazing and beautiful dragon of all. Zulgini, an all-white dragon, was rumored to only saddle the chosen one, and many had tried before Jerreria, but only he had succeeded.

Hoping for someone to say something, he heard a voice come from the back of the chamber. An old man stood and smoked a pipe that gave off different-colored smoke with each puff that he took. His name was Gora, and he was the head of the Council. "Well," he said, "it is of the utmost importance that we deal with this issue right away. The kingdom of Moonrock and the Forest of Angels must be alerted, along with the rest of Arcadia. I shall go to Mount Ora Nak and speak with the Creator. We must all work together to handle such matters."

Jerreria looked at his mentor in hope and relief. If anyone understood him, it was Gora. Gora was his first teacher and had stayed his mentor throughout his years in training as a wizard.

"Jerreria, you shall accompany me to the mountain. Gather your belongings and dragon, and meet me at the Fountain of Life. Council adjourned," Gora said.

Everyone rushed outside the giant Crystal Hall. The hall itself was a magnificent site. It was fixed on top of the Crystal Castle, on the highest point of the highest tower on the castle itself. Some left off the balcony, where they telepathically communicated with their dragons to pick them up. Others left to teach or counsel their underlings while others went to the mess hall for afternoon brunch, for all this chitchat had stirred up quite an appetite. A group of three wizards, though, stayed huddled in the corner. By the looks on their faces, even though no one had noticed, there was mischief brewing, for no one fully knew what was in the heart of any creation, even in Arcadia.

Jerreria entered his quarters in a rush. *I must gather my most important belongings and meet Gora the Galient,* he thought. He grabbed his scroll bag, along with certain amulets and relics he had acquired on his journeys as a youth. He grabbed a jar of Mushramushrooms and another jar of forbidden Jojoa Skunk Weed. Mushramushrooms were weird little mushrooms that seemed to be alive with movement. They were harvested in the deep caves of the Mushra Caverns of Scronopia, and only the dwarves of the region knew where to find them. Not only that but they only appeared every fifteen human years. These mushrooms, when taken with a significant amount of the Jojoa Skunk Weed, allowed a wizard of rank to have visions. Since they tapped into an area of the universe where time didn't exist, and only knowledge did, visions were received not in chronological order but in bits and pieces of the past, present, and future.

Am I forgetting anything? Jerreria thought as he scanned his room. Then with sudden urgency, he turned and motioned the door to close, which did so, because Jerreria had control over material objects in time and space. This was his favorite part. He went to the landing dock for dragons in his tower and ran and jumped off into the clouds. The best way to describe, in our world, what he felt would be like if we were to jump from the highest building built on the highest point.

Speeding downward, Jerreria saw a faint object on the horizon getting closer with speed. *Swoosh*. At lightning speed, he was thrown aside in the air by the great object… Again, *swoosh*. Flying to the other side of the sky, in his mind, he cried out, *Zulgini, this is not the time for games!* Just as he finished thinking that thought, the large, amazing dragon caught Jerreria on his back and smiled in admiration. Both had come a long way and had a long way still to go. Jerreria had Zulgini, and Zulgini had him. They were each other's family and had each other's backs—a connection that went beyond words, to a level of telepathy.

"We must go to the Fountain of Life and meet Gora there. We are on a secret mission of the highest level, so hurry!"

With that thought received, Zulgini replied, "Rushing me, as usual. Did you ever stop to think it is time we take a break from all these missions? It's been a whole century we haven't had one, but at the same time, you know I love an adventure!"

At that moment, Zulgini plunged at full speed downward. Jerreria barely able to grasp his dragon with one hand, and the other on his wizard's hat to prevent it from flying away, seemed to hang on for what seemed like his dear life. Reaching supersonic speed as they dove, the dragon suddenly spread his wings and came to a cruising altitude.

"What is this secret mission, if I may ask, my guardian?" Zulgini asked.

"It has to do with the five scrolls of Arcadia and all the heavens above!" Jerreria replied.

Half a century ago, I felt forces in our world that I had never felt before. I couldn't place my fire on what it was, but now I feel that it is all linked in one way or another, Jerreria, thought the dragon as he focused on his route and adjusted toward the Fountain of Life.

"Much is at stake, my loyal companion, and I feel that it already might be too late."

The dragon roared and thrust forward faster, for he knew Jerreria never worried unless it was of the utmost importance.

CHAPTER 1

Fountain of Life

The Fountain of Life was Arcadia's Shangri-la, or Fountain of ZumZum, for it had mystical healing powers. All of Arcadia's creatures gathered there and drank from the fountain, which came down Mount Ora Nak in a series of wonder-filled waterfalls. It was a majestic site to behold, as if a piece of the heavens above had made its way into Arcadia's blueprint. Different creatures and humanoids drank from the fountain. The white wolves, the golden-antlered and spotted dear, the unicorn, the go-go bird, the Tasmanian tiger, and dinosaurs—three were spotted; one, the flying kind; the other, on two feet; and the last, on all fours with a shield for a head. Also, polar bears and mermaids, along with flying dolphins that had made their way from the Isle of Tantadoha. In the sky above, many beautiful birds and fairylike creatures hovered and danced. You could see the white sun, along with its own moon, and Arcadia's purple one; they all lit the sky, which in turn radiated the most beautiful rainbows. These rainbows illuminated the water as it fell and filled the fountain, perhaps responsible for its healing property.

Zulgini landed near the last fall and drank because this water helped fuel his flame a hundredfold.

"I feel *great*, Jerreria. What do we do next?"

"Zulgini, we wait for Gora—"

Before he could complete his thought, they heard a voice.

"Wait no more, you shall!" Gora said, chuckling, from near the pomegranate pear tree.

"Gora, it has been so long!" Jerreria cried.

"Why, yes, I would say so, because you have grown into a fine young lad."

"Well, I did have the best mentor," Jerreria said as he motioned the tree to uproot and form a seat for his teacher.

Gora, sensing it, sat down. He was frail and much older. He held his staff with both hands when he walked, and he always smiled, emitting the most positive aura. He wore a forest-green wizard's cloak; it was his favorite color. His beard was white as light and his skin brown. He was a great man, and Jerreria admired him much.

"You know what's going on in Arcadia, and I fear my time as head of the Council is short; my bones grow old and my insight frail. The magic makes my joints hurt, and it takes a whole day's rest if I overuse them," he said, shaking his head in grief. Gora motioned to the large branch of the tree to lower so Jerreria could take a seat on it. He then had the tree raise its branch so that the top of Mount Ora Nak was visible. "To the top of the mountain we must go, Jerreria. Collect a few of the pomegranate pears, and let us be on our way. Have your dragon rest here."

Jerreria pointed to a few pomegranate pears and motioned them into his wizard's satchel. As the tree lowered him, he jumped off and started to follow after his mentor, who led the way to the foot of the mountain to begin the long journey upward.

*****

Jerreria, always one step ahead, filled two water bags from the fountain. The fountain was one of the main reasons everyone in Arcadia lived so much longer; it had an antiaging agent, and maybe even more mysterious and wonderful powers that were unknown.

They paved a way through the mysterious forest with just the whim of their thoughts, moving branches and brush aside as they began to discuss a plan of action.

"Jerreria, it is time you earned the staff that awaits you ahead, but you must be worthy of it. If the staff looks into your soul and sees evil, it will destroy you in an instant. If it sees truth and honor, it will uplift you, so to speak," Gora said with a grin. "I learned of its origin when I turned two hundred, and it was a family secret that we have protected for millennia. A sign was given to us that when such events occurred, we should reveal the location to the one whom the Creator is pleased with. I am aware that you are the one spoken of. I wasn't sure when you were a child, but when you reached the age of the dragon, I knew it was you."

The age of the dragon was when a wizard went to the Island of Dragons located on the rim of Arcadia. The journey alone was arduous, but taming a dragon was probably the hardest part. It was a magnificent beast, and only wizards could form a telepathic bond with one, which is why only wizards could ride them. It must be that creature and rider have a mutual bond and respect for each other or an attempt to synchronize could prove fatal consequences for the beast as well as for the rider.

At that moment, Jerreria remembered his first encounter with Zulgini. He could recall every single detail, as if it had just happened. He remembered the moment he peered into the eyes of the teen dragon. It peered back, first with a growl, then turning toward Father Dragon.

Why must I let this humanoid ride me, Father? He is not worthy of our kind in my eyes! he said as he turned toward Jerreria, circling him slowly. Jerreria stood firm and still, keeping his eyes locked on Zulgini.

Son, you came into the world at the same time as Jerreria, for the sun of Arcadia was eclipsed by the star of Nebeustella. It was a wonderful event that marked the year that both you and Jerreria came into existence in Arcadia. Son, it is a sign of greatness to be born on such a day, and a wizard and dragon together are greater than any force in Arcadia. Maybe throughout the whole universe itself, besides our Creator, the One, his father reasoned.

Okay, Father. I understand. Now, how do I tell this thing to get on my back?

Well, you think it to him like I think it to you. I can create a link with any wizard, for I am the oldest dragon, but you, my son, must learn to communicate with your partner. Since the beginning of Arcadia, a truce was made between the first wizard, Abazel, and the first father of all dragons.

You see, first, we came from another world where we were at war, killing one another's races. At that time, we lived off in a faraway system on a water-filled planet, but then

20

one day, we were transported through the tunnel of light and came to Arcadia. Here, we finally joined forces and formed a covenant to end all torture and killing of our races. A prophecy of a wizard was then seen by Abazel himself. He said that a child of his own bloodline would be born on the day of a great eclipse and that he would ride an all-white dragon to fulfill his destiny as the final one to save Arcadia and all the heavens. So form the link, my son.

Looking into Jerreria's eyes, Zulgini spoke with intent toward him, mentally, *Do you hear me?*

Why, of course I hear you. Ha! *I heard you this whole time; I formed the link while you and Father Dragon were telepathing each other.*

Well, get on then! Let us go and see what we can do, Zulgini said as he sped toward the cliff with Jerreria close behind, both diving off as if they had been doing so for years. Jerreria caught up to Zulgini in the nick of time naturally as Zulgini spread his wings to catch an upward lift.

Jerreria was deep in thought, reminiscing about the past, when he was suddenly brought back to reality. "Zulgini is rumored to be the companion of the one who will lead Arcadia in the final battle, but Gora, I am no one special, just a humble wizard who offers servitude to the Most High, Eldest of Elders, the true One and only!"

"And that quality right there is what makes you different, Jerreria! That right there is enough to move mountains, my apprentice." Gora added, "Evil has been whispering in Arcadia, and many have turned to the dark side for powers they choose to pursue. The hearts of men and humanoids are tested and swayed on how the soul drives its vessel. I fear it may be too late, for three of the five scrolls have gone missing and no one knows where they are being hidden. That is why it's time you gain your family heirloom, kept a secret for when light would be needed in dark times.

"The Staff of Abazel, the crystal-powered staff, contains mysterious forces, capable of slicing through anything. Also, it contains the power to bend time and space if mixed with the water from the Fountain of Life. The staff is embedded into the mountain, scourged by the first Father Dragon and Abazel himself so that when the chosen one came, it would be there waiting for him. Only the fire from a pure bloodline along with the chosen one will free the staff from its crystal prison, located at the top and hidden from the naked eye. The fire of the beast at the time must be pure and hot like the core of a supernova, with different colors that blend together with the chosen one's aura to break the mountain's crystal rock of its bonds!"

Jerreria paused. He knew his abilities were above the average wizard's, but never had he dreamt he would be the one to lead Arcadia in its darkest hours. What made him so special or worthy? Maybe it was because he was pure of heart and full of good intention, but was that enough?

Growing up, Jerreria had had no mother and father. They had passed away when he was of a young age. His uncle raised him until it was time for him to become an apprentice. That's when Gora came into his life. Gora taught him the basics in magic, tested him daily, and made him fast for long periods of time under the mystical fall in the Forest of Angels. He made him train physically by catching the crescent moon fairies, the fastest of the fairy race. First, up the mountains near the Crystal Castle then on the wavy waters of the Arcadian Ocean. He also ate different mushrooms and smoked many different weeds to learn the mechanics and understandings of insight, all while having a good laugh and joking along the way. Along with all the physical training, years were spent in the Cave of Hijraruh, where he studied the varied knowledge collected in scrolls handed down through generations and fellowships in Arcadia.

Why a cave? Well, if you wanted to be cut off from the world, what better place was there to be hidden, like a child in his mother's womb? There, you can truly learn, meditate, grasp, acknowledge, and practice all the wisdom that the universe had to offer. Plus, a cave is not a place for fun and games. It is a serious place for serious work to get done without anyone disturbing or distracting from the precious time of attaining academics in a truly scholarly fashion.

CHAPTER 2

The Hidden Evils

T hey had journeyed for a while until they hit the halfway point up the mountain. Jerreria looked at his mentor and knew that Gora was exhausted from the journey even though he didn't want to make it evident. So Jerreria acted as if he was tired and told Gora maybe it was time they called it a day. They made camp, and Jerreria motioned for two pears to make their way to his and his teacher's hands.

As Jerreria started a fire with a snap of his fingers, Gora alerted him in an instant. "Snap out of it, Jerreria, for someone or something approaches us!"

Jerreria immediately motioned for the fire to be extinguished, and they both took on the shapes of forest objects. Jerreria shape-shifted into a boulder while Gora became a tree stump. What a wonderful trick to bend the fragments of light to mimic objects in nature using crystal aura! For one to attain this aura, hard work and long periods of meditation were necessary.

A dragon with dark scales hovered overhead for a second, scanning the area and moving forward as if searching the mountain for someone or something. Once he had moved on, Jerreria and Gora shape-shifted back and looked at each other with concern. It was the feeling in the atmosphere, an intent to kill, a feeling so strong it gave Jerreria chills down his spine.

"Gora, has someone been tracking you since you left the Crystal Castle?" Jerreria asked.

"Well, I'm not sure. My senses aren't what they used to be, my young apprentice."

"I think we have been followed. I felt an odd presence far behind me, from above, when we passed the Forest of Angels. I have never felt such anger or evil intent before. Maybe we are on to something, Gora, and certain elements or people have become aware of our knowledge."

"Well, if that is the case, then let us make haste up the mountain."

Both began anxiously increasing their pace to make it to the top of Ora Nak. Even though the mountain provided Arcadia with the Fountain of Life, the trek to the top was not an easy one. It required much knowledge of the hidden elements, like the crystal sand that swallowed you whole or the poisonous flickerberries that flicked themselves into your mouth and caused instant death. The forest itself was full of traps, from razor blade sharp palm trees that spun in and out of the ground to setting off poisonberry bombs that shot out seeds like bullets as they exploded. The blue leaf of the Hibifus tree could wrap an entire mammoth; it was that big. It emitted a poisonous gas that turned into a mist of acid, melting anything in its way. Each area required knowledge from the scrolls of Mount Ora Nak that Jerreria had memorized, using his photographic memory.

The animals of this forest weren't typical either. They seemed to protect the top of the mountain from strangers and conjurers. One was an ape-like creature, twice as big as a silverback gorilla in our world, with white hairs on his shoulders and running down his back to his lumbar region. Equipt with muscular arms and legs, this creature had the ability to jump straight into the trees in a single leap and break stones with his palms alone. He had also gained enough intelligence to speak in bits and pieces. Another was the saber-toothed tiger, gold-striped with a black coat. He was known to cover the area but wander in and out of it, not allowing anyone to know his true residence. Even in a mystical land, he was a mystical creature.

Closing his eyes and pulling out the scroll from his memories' archives, Jerreria mapped the best trail up the mountain, avoiding pitfalls, crystal sands, and the animals of the forest. Only one with true insight could decipher the path of righteousness that led up the mountain. Putting his hand forward, he said, "Oh light of light, bring forth the illuminated path and shed your light through the darkness!" As he pronounced these words, little figures began lighting up in front of him and Gora. Both began stepping carefully on each lighted spot, which looked like squares inscribed with what seemed like elven hieroglyphics, different from what we are accustomed to seeing on our planet.

"Jerreria, you remembered the illuminated path!" Gora said with pride because he knew he had done well with Jerreria. Gora treated Jerreria like a son because he had been very close to Jerreria's father. They had become apprentices at the same time and used to compete with each other in different areas of magic. After Jerreria's parents passed away, Gora felt an obligation to raise Jerreria as his own son, for Gora had never gotten married. He'd never found time for love because he was so enveloped in the life and art of what it was to be a wizard.

They came toward the end of the illuminated path when a huge chunk of the rocky mountain came crashing down! It landed on the unilluminated part of the track. Both wizards looked at each other with concern, for evil was about to show its face.

Roarrrrrrrrrrrrrrrrrr! came a loud and hissing noise from above, from where they saw a dark-scaled dragon. Gora now recognized whose it was: one of his own. Out of nowhere came Zulgini, crashing into the dragon, yelling mentally to Jerreria, *Jerreria, are you okay?*

Yes, Zulgini. What do you see? Who is attacking us?

It is a dark blue-scaled brother of mine, but I can feel the evil intent it holds within its scales. Take cover as I extinguish its eternal flame forever!

Both dragons began fighting in the sky, back and forth. First with claws ripping at the other's body then, as they flew apart, shooting flames at one another, trying to burn each other out of the sky. In the night sky, at such heights, one might have thought they were firing miniature shooting stars.

On the ground, the piece of mountain rock had set off the series of traps that Jerreria and Gora began blocking and banishing as the threats neared them. The palm trees started to turn, and the humongous Hibifus blue leaf commenced emitting its gas, burning everything in its path. Spears came flying out of the trees from fairies who protected the enchanted place. Forming a bubble of light over himself and

Gora, Jerreria and Gora crossed the treacherous path when in front of them appeared a sinister figure that then spoke.

"Fools, have you no love for your lives?" the stranger said, shooting from his staff an evil magic that was forbidden in Arcadia.

"Abubak, what treachery is this!" Gora exclaimed in anger and resentment.

"For years, you molded and raised Jerreria, neglecting us. All we ever wanted was to be a part of the Crystal Council and learn the depths of the Arcadian Scrolls."

"What have you done, Abubak? Do you understand?"

"I, along with my two cousins, found three scrolls of Arcadia. While you were out teaching your apprentice the ways of the light, we tapped into a stronger energy or force, dark Zusra. Oh, what you failed to teach your student was that the dark forces overpower the light!" he exclaimed as he sent black electricity from his hand toward their shield-of-light barrier, which shattered the shield into millions of light particles.

"How did such evil enter the realm of Arcadia?" Jerreria asked, intense confusion on his face.

"We have learned to channel energy into the land of Arcadia from the realms below, to its deepest level, where the eternal cage of fire holds our master," he answered.

Placing both hands on his staff, he closed his eyes for a split second, reciting what seemed like a language or mantra never heard in Arcadia, *"Hurranashurra bass nafiredo."*

What seemed like black fire came shooting out of the staff and toward Gora.

In an instant, Jerreria grabbed the water from the fountain he had collected and materialized it into what looked like a thin mirror in front of Gora, extinguishing the fire as it ran into it.

"Fist of the hidden mist!" Gora said, as part of the waterfall that was falling beside them turned into a huge fist that came crashing down on Abubak, washing him off the side of the cliff.

CHAPTER 3

Moving Forward

While in the air, fighting the blue-scaled beast, Zulgini noticed a window of opportunity and grabbed the beast by its neck with his razor-sharp teeth. He spun it around and tossed it down toward his master, who had disappeared in the cavern below. No dragon was a match for him. Flying down, Zulgini telepathically asked if Gora and Jerreria were all right. Both nodded in agreement, and Zulgini spread his wings under the waterfall that flowed downward, healing himself of the burns and wounds of battle.

"What do we do now, Jerreria?" the dragon asked his master.

"Gora and I will continue the journey up the mountain. I must acquire the relic trapped in the black crystal prism prison. You scan the area behind us and come around to the front. Make sure the path is clear 'till we reach the top."

Leaping off the cliff, Zulgini spread his wings and took flight, scanning the area for more intruders. Protecting

Jerreria was his destiny, and he was going to see it through to the end.

"Quickly! To the top! Before we have any more interferences. My energy grows weak from battle, and I must fulfill my family's destiny, if it is the last thing I do! Evil must not triumph in Arcadia, for we are the chosen ones who protect the Realm! It is our sworn duty to the universe," Gora said passionately.

Increasing their speed by three times the normal human capacity, they scurried up the mountain and through the forest until they heard a roar like no other! Both froze in their tracks, for they knew what creature had just made its presence known.

CHAPTER 4

Sabretooth Hamza

"Hamza, is that you? You've grown so big!" Gora said, looking into the brush where he'd heard the roar come from. Out came a huge sabertooth, black as stealth, with golden stripes. He snarled, showing his two huge fangs that almost shined in the night.

"I have been hunting in the forests, looking for evil, which I sense is present. Whispers in the trees are of creatures in Arcadia, shape-shifters who have been among us. I saw the white dragon burn his kin out of the sky. I knew something was going on, so I came rushing to see what disturbed the jungle's peace. *Roarrrrrrrrr!* I am born king of this jungle. My father and his father roamed these lands. I shall not be challenged!" Hamza proudly said.

"We are on our way up to get the hidden Staff of Abazel. We must not linger. Time is of the essence," Gora said.

"Okay, then. Jump on my back, Gora. I shall take you up there. It would be my honor, master."

"It has been a while, Hamza. Your father and I would ride together and had many adventures before there was peace in Arcadia. He was a courageous soul. I do see you following in his footsteps. You are to play an important role in all this," Gora said in a calming voice as he positioned himself on top of the enormous creature.

The sabertooth clan was a small one, with only one cub born every five hundred years. Hamza was the current leader and definitely a sight to behold. He was slightly larger than a horse, and his fur was thicker than any normal tiger's on Earth. Two huge fangs exited the top sides of his mouth that could be extended out farther in battle. Hamza could leap over rivers and climb any mountain he set his eyes on. His body was muscular, and he was a war machine when it came to combat. He'd secretly trained with Gora as a cub and sometimes with Jerreria when he was young to help hone their skills.

As they neared the top, they set camp for rest. Jerreria ate his pear as he mentally went through scroll after scroll until he decided it was time to meditate. "Gora, Hamza, I will be back. I shall go meditate with my Mushramushrooms and Weed."

"Don't go far, my apprentice, and only use seventy-five percent of your aura. Leave twenty-five for electromagnetic alertness, in case dangerous frequencies lurk nearby," Gora cautioned him.

Jerreria saw Zulgini sleeping at the foot of the mountain, near the pomegranate pear tree where the waterfall fell. The noise of the water was soothing to dragons, and he often liked to bathe when he awoke after flying all day. Usually dragons were found resting near lakes, rivers, or, in our dragon's case, the Fountain of Life.

"Sleep tight, Zulgini. Tomorrow is another adventure, my companion," Jerreria said to his dragon.

Jerreria walked up a stony cliff and came to a ledge stretched over the cliff side. He sat down and pulled out his pipe and jar of mushrooms as he stared at the moon of Arcadia that blocked the sun at night. It emitted a turquoise light, which was soothing to the soul. It made the sun's moon look like a diamond in the sky, so bright. It was as spectacular as the northern lights in our world but with a few more colors.

He grabbed two Mushramushrooms and tossed them in his mouth, swallowing fast so they wouldn't escape until they'd settled in his stomach. Then he took his long pipe and began to puff large clouds until he closed his eyes and began to see what we would call visions. He saw a large white ape beating its chest. He saw fire and an evil presence in black garments, almost obscured by gray smoke. He saw a prince on a journey and a princess elf in a forest palace. Then he saw a gateway he had never seen before and one eye of a reptilian entity, burning with rage and evil intent.

He opened his eyes and what happened next, he wasn't ready for. Right in front of him, he saw a dragon with a reptilian figure wearing a dark hooded cloak riding it. Jerreria must have put a hundred-percent aura energy into his vision, for in his state of meditation, he didn't even feel such a presence creep up on him.

"Don't you recognize me, Jerreria? Usmak, your master'sss apprentice from before. He neglected us becaussse of you!"

What had happened to Usmak? His body had undergone changes never seen in the realm. Some sort of outside magic had been integrated into his aura, transforming him into a reptilian creature. Before, he was a handsome wizard known among the elven women for his good looks and charm. He was six-foot-three and had dark brown hair with green eyes. His complexion was fair, and physically, he was well built. He always wore glasses though he never needed them, camouflaging himself like a snake would to fit in. Now his new appearance was completely different. Hatred and evil Zusra, which was the dark version of aura and sourced from the realms below, had transformed him into a monster. One could only attain the ability to control Zusra after submitting his or her soul to the evil lord Dajjrah. Usmak had done so. There was no doubt about it.

They began fighting hand-to-hand. Jerreria was good at close-quarters combat, but this creature had more strength and agility than him. Usmak grabbed Jerreria with its tail and flung him against the tree on the cliff. It began to chant something out of the dark scrolls: "*Unagacheehesssyakooo.*" Fire began forming in each palm—a blue fire on one and a yellow one on the other. Usmak combined them and shot it at Jerreria from a crouched position, releasing the flame-like energy at him.

Jerreria put up a hand, using his aura to disperse the dark energy, but it seemed overwhelming, and it overpowered him, unleashing its full force on him.

"Ahhh!" Jerreria yelled in pain, as he kneeled with smoking, fire-scorched garments. "Why, Usmak, would you help evil forces come into Arcadia?"

The reptilian creature began eating off Jerreria's soul energy, sending a red extension of his Zusra, which looked like a cobra with fangs that locked into Jerreria's soul. It began draining him of his life. He then formed a red Zusra sword in his other hand out of thin air. It was as if the sword was a combination of red fire and red electricity, burning bright in the dark night.

"Your time is over. The elder will perish and Dajjrah will be freed just as the Evil Scroll's prophecies explained," Usmak said.

Now close to him, Usmak released the Zusra cobra and took his hood off to show his face. Black, red, and mostly green scales with a yellow neck. Black eyes with no reflection. He opened his skinned hood like a cobra and began hissing as he brought down the blade when a boulder hit him from above, knocking him to the side. A huge white ape stood beating its chest. It was the same one from Jerreria's vision. It was the size of three gorillas, each of his arms a raw pillar of destruction. It yelled "Bad snake!" and threw another boulder that the reptile creature knocked away with its tail.

"Kraynick, transform with my evil Zusra," Usmak said as he sent the Zusra red energy cobra into the dragon, transforming it into a black cobra five times its size.

"Zulgini cannot take on this creature of Usmak, but from the Mushra Scroll, I remember one thing," Jerreria said, putting his hand to his head as if in ultimate concentration, all neurons firing at ten times the normal speed. He scanned the Mushra Scroll in his head and, at the very bottom, saw that if ingested by any other creature, the creature would grow ten times its size for a brief period of time. "King Ape, eat the Mushramushroom!" Jerreria yelled, throwing them toward the ape, guiding them by his hands into his mouth.

The ape began to grow, and it was a battle that almost destroyed the mountain. Two fierce beasts began fighting. The cobra spat venom and fire at the ape as it lunged at him, roaring in anger. Jerreria caught a ride on his leg, climbed up his back, and protected him from the fire before it scorched him with his light aura. He cleared a way and allowed the ape to connect with the creature, taking the battle halfway down the mountain. Jumping off the back of the ape, he telepathically called out to Zulgini, who appeared suddenly, awake from feeling his companion's energy. Jerreria landed on him and told him to take him straight to the top. It was time they collected what was rightfully his.

CHAPTER 5

To the Top

King Ape and the cobra battled gruesomely. The cobra swirled around King Ape and squeezed him tight. Then King Ape, using his arms, loosened the coil of the serpent and freed himself. Beating his chest first, he then transferred all his energy into one humongous blow, hitting the ground and sending out a huge shockwave. It caused the creature to go flying into the forest, destroying the trees and ground, creating a massive crater. Hiding in the snake's mouth, Usmak told him to get in close so that he could strike the beast with his poisoned sword. The creature thrust forward at full speed, spitting Usmak out at the ape and forcing him to land on his face, as he stuck the sword in his right eye.

"AWWW!" roared the king.

Grabbing Usmak and crushing his bones at once, he threw him into the mountain with full strength, shattering every bone in his body. King Ape grabbed two trees and threw them at the snake, but the snake, being an agile creature, missed the first one and then broke the second with his tail as he hissed in anger. It shot venom from its glands, and the acid hit the ape's arm as he protected his face. King Ape yelled in pain and lunged forward, grabbing the snake first by its throat then by its mouth, which he opened with full strength and used to rip the creature in half. What the ape did not know was that this dragon could regenerate itself with some time because of his master's Zusra infused in him.

"Who is that, Gora?" Hamza asked.

"That's one of my students, Usmak. I taught him well and thought he would make a great council wizard one day, but evil was always present within him. I felt it but never acknowledged it, hoping he would change for the better," Gora said. "Let us reach the top fast because I see Jerreria has left King Ape to handle Usmak. I sense him flying to the top with Zulgini above."

At top speed, Hamza the sabertooth ran, leaping through the huge trees and roots that scattered the ground. Though Gora was old, he still had a bit of kick left in him, for his lifetime was nothing short of adventurous. He had conquered the Gretta Beast of Cochonok, and he had saved Arcadia from the Red Witch Queen and her minions. He had reached a level of sage in the ancient mystic arts and was the one wizard who could speak telepathically to anyone in the realm. Over time, he had also mastered the different elements and had been teaching Jerreria how to control air and water but not fire. It was an area that had made much progress toward evil, for it awakened the Zusra within one's consciousness.

"King Ape, are you okay, my old friend?" Gora telepathed to him.

He replied, "Yes, but I need to go to the fountain and heal. Be careful, my friend, for evil has entered Arcadia and we don't know what is going on. Stay at maximum level of awareness at all times!"

*****

Zulgini flapped his wings with great thrusts as he elevated into the clouds and toward the highest point on the mountain.

"Did you feel that, Zulgini?" Jerreria asked, already aware of the answer.

"Yes, Jerreria. What approach would you like to take? Head-on or a more strategic one?"

"I will jump off and glide down to the entrance, where I will enter from the westward side of the mountain through the cave system, toward the top. I felt evil waiting for us there. The ripples of time spoke to me."

Ripples of times were premonitions or déjà vu of the future. Only an attuned person could catch them before they occurred. If this person meditated long enough, he or she could look into the future, glimpses at a time.

Jerreria jumped off Zulgini, leaving him to patrol from the sky, and told him to wait until he sent word for him to flank and attack from above, gaining advantage on his foe. Gliding, Jerreria spoke softly into the wind, causing a slight rise as he made his way around, and then came the fun part. He closed his arms and began a head dive, aiming and angling himself correctly toward the mouth of the cave. Through a narrow cavern with twists and turns, he was like a jet fighter zooming past trees and waterfalls until, all of a sudden, *SWOOSH*! He opened his arms, and the loose garment connected to his sleeves acted like a parachute for his long gown, and he came down softly as a bird. He quickly looked around and entered the cave. Inside, he couldn't see anything, but he kept moving forward. The sound of water droplets from rocks and icicles could be heard, giving it an eerie feeling. Then Jerreria heard something like a scuff of a foot. Then he heard breathing. Then more breaths, which started to turn into growls and coughs.

Jerreria, fearing only his Creator, slammed his hands together and recited an enchantment, "Oh light, giver of life, please provide a beacon in the night." And a miniature star formed which suddenly gave light to what was growling and coughing in the room. It was a horde of evil ogres, but not typical ones. These were elves from the underworld, creatures Jerreria had never come across before. Long black patches of hair stuck to their scalps, as if they were losing their hair. Their skin was gray and slimy. They had vampire fangs and fed on their victims' blood and aura. Along with them stood a giant, who came from the same realm. He was orange in color and had four arms, one held a huge ax, and another a hammer. The other two were for grabbing, if our hero got too close.

What came after was complete execution. Jerreria froze and used the ripples of time to mentally create a plan of attack. As the ogres came near and the first claw was about to touch his shirt, it was as if lightning struck them. He was so fast that no eye in our world could have caught it. He only had one second of time in hyper mode, and he executed perfectly. All the vampire ogres near him were taken out. The first one, he hit in its stomach, as the one next to him got an uppercut. Following each move, executed as gracefully as a ninja would, he performed a sweep move. The evil creatures' chests were crushed with his staff, and they received blows to their temple's and fontanelle's, discombobulating them completely. The iron fist of the monks in our world was just a scratch on the surface of the strength Jerreria exhibited at that very moment.

"Sage fist of Arcadia!" He put his hands together and built a wind-like fireball that he charged up and released, throwing his open palms toward the giant and knocking him backward. This caused him to trample over the evil elves, knocking them out, or at least the ones that were left standing. The giant, in rage, slammed both of his weapons into the earth, causing the ground to break apart, the force of the blow speeding toward Jerreria.

Jerreria, aware of his strength, thought he could easily block such a force until it struck him. The giant was using dark energy to make his attacks stronger; Zusra raged in his eyes. Jerreria snapped his arm back into place. He then grabbed his staff and started to spin it. He let it go, but the spinning continued to increase until sparks of electricity began to appear in its circular trek. The electricity sparked into lightning that lit up the whole room. He threw it at the giant who deflected it and rampaged forward. Jerreria ran at him, sliding through his legs just as the giant struck down and came up on the other side of him. Then Jerreria used precise two finger hits to certain pressure points and lymph nodes in the giant's chakra system. Paralyzing one leg, he grabbed the brute's arm and flipped himself up into the air to land on the giant's shoulders where he delivered two fingered hits to the jugular veins and two elbows to the top of the head. The giant fell and passed out, and Jerreria landed on the ground, flipping gracefully from the giant's shoulders onto the cave floor. The evil minions were strong but had no chance against our hero, for he played an important role—for all Arcadia and all mankind.

Jerreria ran up the caverns until he neared the top, where he slowed his pace. He made his way to the entrance, where death had been waiting patiently for his arrival. The battle between good and evil was about to begin, and this was the start of the prophecy we were all forewarned about.

CHAPTER 6

_{ᘏᖆᖇ}

Isra

"Jerreria, I have been waiting for you. Don't be shy. It has been years since I have seen you."

Isra was the youngest but most capable of the three of Gora's apprentices. He was short and quiet, and he mostly kept to himself. He had pale white skin and was slightly younger than Jerreria. Now he was an evil, faceless entity consumed by the evil Zusra. He was in a hooded black cloak with darkness for a face, and he had skeleton-like arms covered in black armor.

"Isra, why are you here?" Jerreria asked him. "There is danger. Usmak and Abubak are near and are dealing with dark magic energy."

"Oh really, Jerreria? How is it that you have come to know about dark magic energy, when all you did was follow Gora around like a little dragon does its mother? Gora making you his favorite left us in the shadows to figure things out for ourselves. Ahhh!" Isra turned around and moved a huge boulder, sending it hurtling toward Jerreria, who countered it with aura from his left hand, holding it back but with much effort.

Out of nowhere came Abubak with a maroon Zusra sword in his hands, ready to strike. Jerreria, with a flash of energy, moved out of the way of Abubak's strike.

Even though these were his fellow apprentices, they had hated and despised him from the beginning. They'd always picked on Jerreria, though he didn't fight back nor even say a word to Gora. He was the chosen one, at least that was what everyone whispered, and that jealousy created evil within their hearts. Time after time, they tried to make Jerreria the laughingstock of all the wizards. They lied and passed around false rumors, set traps for him, and even put bean fairy dust in his clothes, which caused him to smell like farts and flowers.

Isra appeared behind Jerreria and delivered a blow, black electricity in his fist. He then lifted Jerreria's body by raising the earth beneath him with such force that it flung him into the air. Isra, still controlling the boulder, sent it at full speed, catching Jerreria and forcing him to collide into the mountain wall and be squashed.

Just as impending death was at its closest, a voice came from behind them.

"You all always picked on Jerreria, even when he never did anything to harm you. That is why I chose to train him and not all of you." Motioning the rock to fall, Gora said, "Stay where you are, Abubak." The nefarious Abubak now appeared to be stuck in some sort of time trance.

"Jerreria, find Zulgini at once and free the Staff of Abazel," Gora instructed him.

"You never favored us, but our new lord does, master!" Isra yelled in anger.

"Is that why you cover your face, Isra, and only show your eyes when necessary?"

"If I showed you my face, you wouldn't recognize me. The dark Zusra is more painful to attain. I suffered many wounds from the purple electricity until I learned to harness it, and my dark lord Dajjrah showed me how," Isra said. Putting both hands together in the air, he summoned a dark cloud that started fueling him with dark electricity.

"No matter how far down that path you have gone, you can always turn around, Isra. You were like my child once. You don't have to do this," Gora gently coaxed.

"It is not me who wants this done. My lord commands it—your energy as a sacrifice to Dajjrah."

Letting all the electricity shoot out of his hands at Gora, he completely obliterated the old man.

"Neat trick. I never taught you, you foolish, misled child." Gora appeared from behind the rock, and another version of him appeared from around a tree. The last version came flying out of the sky, and they all attacked at once.

Isra became overwhelmed, but he was the angel of death and was able to be in many places at once. At once, he began forming portals that he appeared in and out of, all the while fighting Gora's clones. Abubak, finally freeing himself from the trance, was about to aid Isra in his battle when he heard a growl from behind him. He turned around to see Hamza jump at him. Quickly, Abubak turned into a black bear, and the two began to fight back and forth ferociously. The battle lit up the top of Ora Nak.

Usmak, camouflaged, saw a window of opportunity to attack and came out of the mountain cavern and began reciting an evil mantra as he looked into Hamza's eyes. It put him in a trance, and he fell over, dazed. Then, Abubak transformed back into his human form and joined Usmak in the evil mantra. They started forming dark energy in each hand and quickly took out the clones that Gora had created to assist him. At that point, Isra joined in the mantra.

"*Ujanavaojaoka low,*" they chanted. These were words no one in Arcadia understood except for them, for they had learned them from their new lord. Gora's energy began to leave his body, and all three started feeding on it.

"We will sacrifice you, master, for our lord. Your energy will help free him from his cage," Isra said.

Just as Gora gave his last sigh, a huge flame came at laser speed and knocked Abubak off the mountain top. Then came Jerreria, gliding in and knocking Usmak off the side of the mountain where he stood.

"Combined light-fire cosmic blast!" Jerreria shot white electricity combined with Zulgini's fire like a laser beam across the mountain at Isra in a killing blow, when out of nowhere a warp hole opened, and he disappeared in a flash. The beam missed Isra and destroyed the structure directly behind him.

Isra, at the time, just happened to be standing in the middle of the summit right next to the crystal prism. It was a black crystal rock structure that had now melted away like lava, and in it, a staff was visible: the Staff of Abazel! It was white with crystalline trimming and some engraved text in a language that Jerreria recognized as ancient script; it was unlike any other staff. Two crystals rotated like planets around the main crystal that was precisely positioned on the top. The scripts began to glow. He looked at it in amazement, but instead of admiring it, he went to his mentor's side.

"Jerreria, I'm so glad I get to see you one last time. My energy has left my body, and I can feel it all gone. I want you to know one thing before I go: You are going to be put through the hardest test of your life. I hope I did well in my task of preparing you, my son—" Gora's words were cut short from his wheezing and coughing. Clearing his throat, he continued, "The Creator watches over you. I hope I lived up to the promise I made to your father. No matter what happens, do not fall into the Zusra, the dark side of magic controlled by Dajjrah, your nemesis and eternal enemy. Take the staff. I put the last of my energy into it for a time you might need to call on me."

Gora's body then began turning into light and vanished into the atmosphere. Jerreria let out a cry and then went running to the crystal staff. This was what was left of his master, and he was going to learn to control it, no matter what.

"Let us go, Zulgini. We have much to report."

"Jerreria, I'm so sor—"

"Forget it. Let us just do what is most important now: Save Arcadia and find the last two scrolls."

With a nod, Zulgini took off into the night sky and so began the search for the Scrolls of Arcadia!

CHAPTER 7

The Princess

In a distant forest, two elven figures rushed through the treetops, landing from branch to branch without making a noise.

The Forest of Angels was a majestic forest, full of life and mystery. It was home to the elves of Arcadia, where King Elvin was ruler of them all. His daughter, Aurora, was the princess and heir to the throne, for she was an only child and it was her blood right. She was tall and slender with long golden hair that fell to her knees. Her green eyes seemed to hold a whole ocean in them; her gaze was mesmerizing, and you could get lost in it as days passed. She was the most beautiful female in all Arcadia. This was a well-known fact. Aurora's field of expertise was green aura energy, which was used for healing. She had come a long way from her teenage years and was now able to heal major wounds. She also was very confident and strong. Her father had her trained by his personal guard, and they were the best in combat in the Forest of Angels.

"Hurry up, Gadlin!" Princess Aurora said as she passed by him in a flash.

"I am trying, but I am no match for my princess!" Gadlin said with a laugh as he tried to keep up.

Higher in the mountain treetops, they made their way until they came to their destination: a cove with a special pond illuminated by fireflies that flew in all directions.

"The Cove of the Fairy Tree!" Aurora exclaimed in happiness, for her father had always taken her there for training when she was young. They settled and began to enjoy fairy cakes.

"Did you hear about what happened at Mount Ora Nak last night, Aurora?" Gadlin asked with curiosity.

The truth was that she had overheard her father talking to his council after word had reached them of the battle at the top of the mountain. Evil forces in Arcadia were disturbing the peace because it was the last line of defense before the heavens themselves. It had been centuries since evil had made its way into the realm, and now the new generations had to face what villains lay ahead.

"The death of Gora the Galient is truly a loss for all Arcadia. The evil one—dare I say his name—is already halfway free, with three of the scrolls under his control. The time is now to take action, but father doesn't have the slightest clue where to begin," Aurora said, answering her friend's question.

"Perhaps we should take the initiative and set out on a journey to save Arcadia!" Gadlin said as he jumped up and started mimicking battle moves like an elven warrior, his sword swinging as if to strike blows to his enemies.

Gadlin was a strong young elf. His gray hair and blue eyes made him look older than he really was. With his masculine figure, he was trained in archery and elven blades like his forefathers, the warrior elves. Gadlin's father had served King Elvin all his life on his council and had died protecting the royal family. For this reason, Aurora's father had Gadlin assigned to protect Aurora, and since their teenage years, he had done a good job.

"Maybe we should ask your father. We can't just sit around and wait for the enemy to strike. Right, Aurora?"

"Right, but Father is overwhelmed. Why don't we wait for a better time to approach him, when he will really listen to us."

She always had a way of making the best out of a situation; it was her job as a princess. Once they finished their cakes, before it got dark, they started their journey back to the wooden castle.

As they crossed the great river from above, they saw a familiar sight.

"Zulgini!" Aurora exclaimed with happiness. She knew if Zulgini was there, then so would his master be.

"Jerreria finally makes an appearance in our forest," Gadlin said with a little jealousy in his tone, for he knew Aurora had taken a liking to Jerreria. What elven woman wouldn't?

"Quick! Let's hurry back! I don't want to miss what he and father are to talk about!" the princess told her Gadlin.

Both rushed onward, eager to hear any news of the new evils in Arcadia.

*****

The dwellings of the forest elves were a site to behold. The architecture was seldom seen because not everyone was welcome there. The trees rose hundreds of feet, with embedded carvings of past warriors, kings, and queens. Parts of the great river broke into little rivulets that ran through and brought life to the area. Staircases were widely distributed with bridges in the treetops that joined the housing network above. Elves felt more comfortable in the treetops than in the forest below. The king's living quarters were in the middle of everything, weeping willow-like leaves forming a curtain and offering refuge from intrusive eyes.

"Zulgini, drop me off here. I shall call on you once the meeting with King Elvin is over. Please keep a lookout for anything out of place, and notify me at once if you see anything of concern." Jerreria then took flight and glided down into the wooden palace of the king.

"Jerreria, we have been waiting for your arrival," one of the five councilmen who had gathered in the throne room said.

"Well, I hope I did not keep you waiting too long," Jerreria replied.

"Not at all, my friend," the king said, entering the room and making his way to the throne to take his seat.

"Sir, we have urgent matters to discuss. Evil has arisen in Arcadia, and we must take action at once." Then, peering around the room, he said, "May we talk in private, Your Highness?"

"Only if I may join the conversation," Aurora said as she entered the room with a tired Gadlin behind her.

"Very well. Everyone leave us be, as we discuss further matters," the king said. When everyone was gone, he turned to our hero. "Well, Jerreria, what is it?" the king asked, concerned.

"Sir, three of the five scrolls have been taken in Arcadia, and we must prevent the last two from falling into the wrong hands or we all will perish, and the heavens above will be compromised."

"Father, what scrolls does Jerreria talk about?" the princess asked, eager to know.

"Jerreria, do you care to explain to Aurora the history of the scrolls?"

"Once the Creator created the universe and all the creatures in it, he enclosed the evil one Dajjrah in an eternal cage of fire for going against his word but allowed him to have a window in his cage from which he could try to test all creations.

"The knowledge of all eternity was cast into these five scrolls and given to the elders in Arcadia, who took it upon themselves to hide and secure each one. If put together, the five scrolls could make a person's wish come true. One was given to the wizards and one to the elves. One to the dragons and one to Elanor, the Queen Mermaid. The last scroll's whereabouts are unknown. King Elvin's scroll, the wizards', and Elanor's have been taken through trickery and treachery. Intelligence of each scroll was found or taken through means of greed or temptation to further the ends of man, wizard, elf, or mermaid.

"Only the dragons' scroll remains because they are on the outskirts of Arcadia and do not meddle with other beings besides wizards, and they have been able to keep their scroll safe until now. I am having visions of gathering a team, one person from each clan of people. I, the wizard, and Zulgini, my dragon, represent our kinds. I would like for you, Sir, to allow Aurora to join my journey, for I saw her in my vision, along with a prince riding a great lion like an elven horse. I am to gather these individuals and find the last scrolls before Usmak, Abubak, or Isra do. The one I dare not mention cannot be freed from his cage of fire or all the heavens will be compromised."

"There always comes a time in one's life when they must choose the well-being of others over their own. It is a task only royalty can perform." The king turned to his daughter and asked, "Aurora, my daughter, are you willing to join Jerreria on his journey for the last two scrolls and promise to represent the elves in this alliance of Arcadia?"

"Yes, Father. I am. If this is my destiny and my story, I shall not let the elves down and will have the elders write of our courage in the chronicles of Arcadia."

"I would like Gadlin to accompany you. He has always protected you," King Elvin said with pride.

"Father, I am of age and don't need a guard by my side," the princess protested.

"I agree with Aurora, Your Highness. However, I will honor your word and let him come with us as far as the Island of Dragons. I cannot let the last scrolls be compromised," Jerreria said.

"Agreed, Jerreria. You do not yet know the burden of a father." He looked at Aurora as if it were the last time he would see her.

"Then let us gather our strength and leave at the break of light. I will go smoke at the Cove of the Fairy Tree and meditate on things," Jerreria said with concern as he exited the room with urgency.

CHAPTER 8

The Adventure Begins

In her chambers, Aurora was excited. She had never really been on an adventure let alone one that would decide the fate of Arcadia. Her father had told her that they would have a huge elven feast for her before she departed in the morning.

Elves knew how to put together a banquet indeed. The throne room had been turned into a dining hall where fairy wine, bread, and cake were spread across the table. Different fruits from the forest were there as well, including blue apples and orange and red bananas. Tiny grapelike watermelons, green berries, and yellow berries were on display. All the elves had gathered and were having a great time. Cups clanked, and friends sang along with the stories of warriors from days past. King Elvin, sitting next to his beautiful queen, raised his glass. "To my daughter, Aurora. May the One, the Creator, protect you on your adventure to save the realm and the heavens above. Yahhh!" He raised his cup in admiration and pride. "And," he continued, "Gadlin will accompany Aurora until the Island of Dragons. Your father protected us with his life, and I only trust Aurora's with you, Gadlin."

"I will be honored to do so, Your Highness," Gadlin said, taking a knee and placing his right arm on his chest and heart.

Across the hall, our wizard and his dragon entered as special guests.

"Well, I guess tonight is a true night for celebration, right, Zulgini?" Jerreria said upon entering the room, to everyone's surprise as usual.

"Right you are, Jerreria!" Zulgini said as he flew up and into the sky, round and round, creating a fire show for everyone to enjoy.

The party continued, with fairies providing the music through the night until it was time for everyone to retire.

In the morning, everyone gathered at the wooden city's entrance to bid the princess farewell. Dressed in her elven armor of white steel and gold, along with silver trimming, Aurora made her way on her white elven horse through the crowd. Her father's sword hung on her right side, and the bow on her left side was folded away. Every elf knew archery and swordplay, as it was a tradition passed down from warrior to warrior. In battle, they could call upon their weapons to form in their hands, for each one was enchanted. Aurora was highly trained in archery, the best in her class.

"Aurora, wait for me," Gadlin said as he rode up from around the corner, bidding his friends and family goodbye.

From his castle perched in the treetops, the king watched with his queen as their only child left their nurturing forest.

"I have dreaded this day for a long time," the king said with a sigh as a tear formed in the corner of his eye.

"Oh, Elvin, didn't you see how happy she was? Just like her father, ready for an adventure," the queen comforted him.

"But what she will face is what I fear. The evils have shown their faces, and this may be the battle we have heard of in our prophecies."

"If so, may the One protect her on her journey."

Aurora and Gadlin, on their elven steeds, ran across the open field as they left the dense forest trees. Racing each other as always, they both ducked a little as Zulgini flew past them overhead. Looking at each other, they motioned for their elven horses to run faster, in fear of being left behind by the great dragon.

CHAPTER 9

The Tribe of the Barbarians

Jerreria looked for a spot on the side of the mountain in the Hunganan Pass for everyone to rest. He began to set up camp and motioned Zulgini to bring the princess and her friend because horses couldn't travel to the spot Jerreria had chosen. Jerreria took some star dust and sprinkled it into his tea. He lit his pipe with his premade mixture of Mushramushrooms and began to meditate.

In his visions, he saw warriors of great strength training for battle. Instead of riding horses, they rode lions and had huge swords the length of their bodies. One young lad stood out from the rest, and behind him was an entity full of fire, but it gave him mixed signals. It looked like the warrior demon Kattz from the Warrior Scroll.

"Jerreria! Why did you leave us behind like that?" Aurora asked as Zulgini came in and landed on the edge of the entrance to the cave.

"I am sorry, princess, but I thought it wise that I scout ahead in case danger was present and find a safe place for you to rest your eyes for the night," Jerreria replied.

"Jerreria, I am starving. Do you have any fairy cakes or dwarven ale?" Gadlin asked, hungry from the long day's travel.

"Why, of course! I magically prepared a feast for us," he said and motioned the fire to blaze higher, which showed plenty of Arcadian food on an elven blanket ready to be devoured.

They sat on the edge of the cliff after the great meal and enjoyed a smoke and some tea before they retired for the night. Even in such hard times, good company made the worst of it seem better.

*****

As the sun began to rise, so did Arcadia's champions. They had their breakfast, and Jerreria jumped off the cliff, gliding through the mountain pass, telepathically telling Zulgini to drop off the princess and her guardian at their horses and catch back up with him before he lost too much altitude. Zulgini smirked because everyone in Arcadia knew he was the fastest of all dragons.

Jerreria, just use your wind magic to give you an upward lift, like when we fought the flying creature of Locnardia who was attacking all the griffons. Remember? Zulgini told his master through telepathy.

Yes, but I was flying on your back before I learned wind magic my companion, and I feel more comfortable with you around. To be honest, there is no one I trust more with my life, he thought back.

"I know, and I like hearing you think it. I'll be back faster than I can breathe fire. Oh, by the way, what is our objective right now? You never told me of your vision." Swooshing his wings with force, he disappeared into the sky.

Well, we are here to recruit our warrior. Aurora is our healer, but we will be facing an army of evil creatures. We must have a sword-bearer on our side. The universal conscious knows what is necessary, and we must follow our instincts, for each vision is a piece of the puzzle, dear Zulgini! Whizzing through the pass like a jet fighter, our wizard saw Barbaria ahead.

CHAPTER 10

Aliya, the Warrior Prince

In the Evil Forest, a figure in a black cloak motioned a pack of wolves into a huge black tree that opened up and led them into a large cult-like throne room. On it sat Abubak, with Usmak at his side.

"I spoke to our evil lord, and he has commanded that we begin the attack. First, we must take care of Gora's apprentice and the alliance he is assembling," Abubak announced.

Usmak, hissing in happiness, said, "Once captured, bring them back here so I can eat them and enjoy their life energy!"

"Let us begin forming our warriors. The wolves have decided to join our side, so let us give them the evil Zusra," Abubak said as he motioned for the other two to encircle the wolves. Then they began the incantation.

The wolves transformed and grew larger until they stood on their hind legs with huge, large claws and muscular bodies. Medieval armor formed over their bodies, and medieval weapons appeared in their hands, swords and axes created for their size and mass.

The alpha wolf, now transformed into a lycan, was all black with yellow eyes. His name was Tachakra, and he was a strong creature. He growled and started to walk toward the exit. Looking back, from the side, he snarled, "Consider it done. Say no more!" And the pack ran out at high speed through the Evil Forest and in the direction of our heroes.

*****

Zulgini had caught up with Jerreria, and they landed in the town of Barbaria. It looked more like a war campsite, for barbarians liked living in large tents. Jerreria passed through the town, watching the warriors train. Some were learning to ride their lions, and others were practicing the long sword, a barbarian's weapon of choice. Others were throwing a sling with three balls on it to trap the enemy's legs and tie them up, disabling them for the killing blow.

He made his way through the market and the lion stables, from where they were led to the king's palace tent. Though it was a tent, it was a magnificent site. Two white lions in armor guarded the entrance. Jerreria felt a bit nervous passing the two beasts as he went in. Though the lions of

Barbaria were larger in size, comparable to a horse on earth, Hamza the sabertooth was larger and stronger than them all.

In the palace, hookahs producing different-colored smoke were being used. Two large tables ran along each side of the hall, where everyone gathered and ate as a clan. The tent was filled with rugs and furs. The king sat on a huge throne next to his barbarian queen, who was known throughout the land for her beauty. The king wore a huge white cloak of fur, and so did all his warriors but of different sorts and in different styles.

He saw Jerreria and beckoned him forward. "What is a wizard doing in Barbaria? It has been ages since one has set foot in my land," King Hizraz said as he motioned his guard to bring Jerreria a chair and seat it next to him.

"Times of conflict, my king, brings me to your land. I am in search of a mighty warrior who will accompany me on the quest for the hidden scrolls," Jerreria whispered.

"And how is Gora, Jerreria?" the king asked.

"No longer with us," Jerreria replied, looking straight ahead.

"I see. This quest must be of the utmost importance, if Gora the Galient has fallen," the king said sternly.

"I need your best warrior," Jerreria said, now looking directly at the king.

"Let us hold a competition, then—"

As the king was finishing his sentence, a guard rushed into the tent. "On the northeast side, Your Highness, two elves—a female and a male—were attacked by large wolflike creatures on two legs. They captured them and started heading toward the direction of the Evil Forest."

"Princess Aurora!" Jerreria, concerned, exclaimed.

"Well, Jerreria, this will be the factor that decides your warrior," the barbarian king said, looking at him, then turning to his people, he said, "Whichever one of my warriors brings back the princess and her guard shall have the honor of accompanying Jerreria on the quest for the hidden scrolls and making a name in Arcadian history as the barbarian who helped save all Arcadia! Whowah!" he yelled as everyone replied back with their own "Whowah!"

As this was happening, no one had noticed that the young Prince Aliya was no longer in the hall. He was already on his way with Zulkirnaan, his dreaded sword, on his back. With a long black ancient steel in the center, and silver lining that had another language inscribed on it, something elven and ancient, this was no ordinary blade. It was split at the end to inflict more damage, and inside, some angelic warrior demon soul, Kattz, was trapped. It glowed hot like lava with the writings also glowing. Both Aliya and his mighty sword were ready for battle. Nothing would stand between him and the princess.

CHAPTER 11

~~~~~

The Battle of Zedon

Aliya held on tightly to his lion's mane. It was all white, like his parents' which stood outside the palace tent and guarded the king and queen. Ragnor was a strong and ferocious creature with light blue eyes. He was huge in size and had muscular limbs for tearing and ripping when necessary. He'd been given to Aliya when he turned five, and both had made fun and created mischief while growing up. Though they did not have a telepathic connection, they communicated through animal instinct.

I must save the princess and show Father I am a worthy warrior of our clan, he thought to himself as he sniffed the air for the scent he had been following. He was able to track the evil Zusra because it was a foreign energy to his land. He knew that by nightfall, he would be near the campsite of the enemy. Fury in his eyes, he saved it for the time of battle. Aliya was a berserker. If enraged, he would go into a mode of fury where no one was safe. Anything and everything would be annihilated, and, in that moment, his rage would ignite Zulkirnaan, his sword. Forged by the dwarves of Mushra Mountain, in the lava rivers below, the mystical lava stored the mythical fire energy within the sword itself. The sword had two points at its end instead of one and was much larger than all other swords in Barbaria. Though he was only a teen entering manhood, in Arcadia, he was faster and stronger than most of his clansmen. He had long dark-brown hair tied in a ponytail that fell to the curvature of his back. His skin was dark gold, and he stood a good seven feet in height. His body was extremely chiseled, and he was the most handsome of any creature in the realm.

Tachakra ordered the rest of the lycans to stop and set up camp. He placed the princess and her guard down against a tree and told the others to patrol the area and eat one of the horses. He sat at the fire, eating Aurora's horse's leg and began talking.

"Now, why does the dark lord want a mere elf? I don't understand. Better I eat you instead," he said, laughing and snarling lightly as he finished the leg and then moved on to sharpen his blade.

"Is that whom you take orders from? The dark lord?" the princess asked in anguish.

"We take orders from our masters, the three sorcerers," Tachakra replied.

"What drove you creatures to turn to the dark side?" Aurora asked.

"We were tired of being mere creatures. We wanted more power, and only the sorcerers could give us that."

The princess, looking up at the Arcadian moons, hoped that help was on the way.

Slowly stepping from branch to branch, Aliya made his way toward the camp. He was an excellent tracker and had found the lycans' campsite. One lycan walked underneath his tree, and, in a flash, he fell upon him and, with his gigantic sword, brought down the lycan. Another one nearby heard a slight noise from Aliya's first encounter and was met with a silent slash from a cloaked warrior. Aliya jumping back up into the trees, sniffed the air for more enemies.

"Sir, I just found Baka and Naka dead," one lycan reported to Tachakra.

"Everyone, spread out. I want this thing or person caught and brought back to me."

The pack disappeared in all directions.

Tachakra felt a nearby presence and began sniffing the air. Aliya was getting closer to the camp, and just as he was nearing, Tachakra grabbed him from behind. "Well, look who we have here. Awwoooooooooooo!" All the lycans came running.

Aliya was held by the lycans' mouths, clenching onto his arms and legs. They also caught Ragnor and chained and caged him as he roared back at them.

"What are you, creatures, and what do you want with the princess?" Aliya asked in pain from being held by each werewolf.

"You are in no position to ask questions, barbarian!" Tachakra yelled. "Arcadia's end is near, and we will free our master soon enough," the alpha continued.

"Not if I can help it," Aliya said in a low voice as his eyes started to turn fire-red and his veins began to bulge.

"Hold him tight. Do not let him move!" Tachakra yelled, feeling the power building within Aliya.

As Aliya began breathing deeper, his sword began to glow red like lava was around its edges.

The wolves' mouths started to burn, and they had to let go. In that moment, Aliya was in berserk mode, swinging his sword with accuracy and moving lightning fast. It was a complete massacre; every wolf was put down by the burning Zulkirnaan. Tachakra fled, barely escaping.

As the prince neared the elves, the princess began to chant a healing spell. As he came closer, he began to slow and lose his anger until he fell at her feet. Both elves used Aliya's sword to free themselves, and they also released Ragnor. They put Aliya on Ragnor's back, and themselves got on Gadlin's steed. Now free, they started heading toward Barbaria. Along the way, they were met by the king's warriors and everyone who had set out to save them.

They all made camp and held a feast in honor of the prince and princess. After Aliya awoke, he was seated next to Aurora at the king's table. The two looked at each other and smiled. They had just survived their first encounter with evil in Arcadia, and Aliya had proven to his clan that he was a worthy warrior. After dinner, the king announced his son as the representative of the barbarians on the quest for the hidden scrolls of Arcadia.

Everyone exclaimed in joy, and Jerreria smiled.

His fellowship was growing stronger.

CHAPTER 12

The Alliance

After the celebrating and the wrestling and the lion matches, Jerreria called upon everyone at his campsite. Aliya came with Ragnor, Zulgini landed after surveying the area, and Gadlin rode up on his steed.

"Where is Aurora?" Jerreria asked, looking at Gadlin.

"She said she was freshening up a bit and heading this way."

"I see. Well then, what I wanted to begin with is—"

"A big thank you to our hero, Aliya!" the princess said, walking up and laughing as her eyes gleamed while looking at the prince.

Gadlin was confused because he rarely saw the princess like this. He looked away in dismay; it bothered him that he had been unable to defend her the moment the creatures had overcome them. Meanwhile, Jerreria looked surprised himself because elves always loved and married elves, but he felt her energy for him, and though he did not know its depth, it was indeed love. And why not? Aliya was a prince, the most handsome of all barbarians. His height and strength made him admirable to all women. He, though, was quiet and reserved; he spent most of his time training with Zulkirnaan and Ragnor or alone in the wilderness. He wanted to be the greatest warrior Arcadia had ever seen and knew little about emotions like love. He saw how the princess occasionally looked and smiled at him. Usually, when women showed any interest in him, he thought nothing of it. This time, it was different. He felt her energy almost reaching out to him. He looked down to the ground, trying to rid himself of such thoughts.

Jerreria began by saying, "We are the fellowship on the quest for the lost scrolls. Three of five are in the hands of the evil sorcerers of Dajjrah. Our quest is to find the remaining two and stop their conjuring. We must figure out what they plan to do with the scrolls, though I am afraid I already have an idea."

The scrolls attained all knowledge of the Arcadian library. All knowledge of the universe was split into the scrolls and Dajjrah would only get one thing from gathering them: freedom.

"Aliya, you are our warrior and will protect and fight for us, especially for the princess. She is our healer and is of royal bloodline."

Aurora, pleased with what Jerreria had said, smiled at him bashfully.

Aliya, petting Ragnor, who lay next to him, said, "It would be my honor, Jerreria. My Zulkirnaan swings for Arcadia and all the heavens."

"What is our next step then, Jerreria? Now that we have assembled, what do we do?" Zulgini thought to his companion.

"Next, I will go to Elanor, the queen mermaid of the Isles of Tantadoha and Atlantia, leader of all sea creatures. I must inquire about the whereabouts of the last two scrolls. I would like for you to gather one fairy from the Island of the Hidden Mist of Ziona for our quest. They always come in handy in dire times. Aurora, take Zulgini while I am away. He will protect you and guard you, along with our prince," Jerreria instructed.

Everyone finished their tea, which Jerreria had prepared with different herbs, and headed to their tent for a night's rest.

In the morning, the alliance gathered their things, and everyone set out in their own direction. Jerreria had been meditating with the Staff of Abazel, and his powers had been getting stronger. He had Zulgini take him to a high altitude before he glided off toward the isles.

Aliya sheathed his sword to Ragnor and looked at the princess as she finished tying the cloak she had received from the Queen of Barbaria the night before at dinner as a gift. She was different. *Maybe this journey will be a good way to get to know her*, he thought as he jumped on Ragnor and yelled "Yahh, Ragnor!" his lion roaring and taking off with all his speed.

Gadlin came galloping behind on his black stallion almost as if trying to race the prince through the open field. Aurora, now on Zulgini's back, watched the prince gazing as if lost in thought. He had released her from danger that night at Zedon but had captured her heart at the same instant. The thought of journeying with him brought joy to her chest, and her heart beat in excitement. She giggled to herself at the thought of falling in love with a barbarian. Aliya was a peculiar man indeed, one she wanted to get to know better.

Adventures always had a funny way of forming love between a prince and a princess, and this tale would prove that Aliya and Aurora were a match made in the cosmos, their destiny written ages ago in the stars.

CHAPTER 13

A Bond Called Love

Tachakra leaned in toward the river to drink and saw Isra appear in the water. Isra had the look of the Grim Reaper, no face to be seen with a dark smoke or mist that hung about him. The sight of him always gave Tachakra a cold chill down his spine.

"Where is the princess?" Isra asked in a deadly tone.

"A barbarian came and saved her. He went into a berserk rage and killed my pack! All of them!" he snarled, punching the earth and shaking the rocks around him.

"Track them and stay close. When the time is right, I shall send reinforcements to aid in her abduction. She is an important piece of our plan, so she must be apprehended," Isra told Tachakra.

"I shall not fail you again." After speaking, he took off running in the direction of the princess, her scent still in his nostrils.

Tachakra knew that if he didn't listen to his master, he would lose the power he'd been granted. He often saw the humanoids walking on two legs speaking to one another. He wanted to know what it was like to be one of them. All his life, they had been slaves to the other kind—on earth, pulling their sleds, hunting their prey and beaten and abused at times. He wanted to know what it was like to *be* them, in a more powerful position. They always felt separated in society. Everyone walked on two legs above them while they walked on all fours.

Now they had a chance to do it differently but not without a cost. Instinctively, he had an urge to kill, but something in him also wanted to protect. He ran through the forest into an open field and up the mountain, where he stopped to howl at Arcadia's moons. As the moonlight struck him, his mane grew bigger and his muscles larger. It seemed the moonlight had made him stronger and faster. He plunged off the mountaintop, taking large leaps, covering a mile or two at a time.

Tearing through the woods, he used his claws like machetes, his razor-sharp nails having no trouble. He climbed up a large tree and went to the top, searching for Aurora's scent, which had moved into the air.

She must be airborne, he thought as he jumped through the trees.

*****

Behind the waterfall, they awoke together at once as the sunlight seeped in through the water. Gadlin galloped up to the entrance and yelled for them. He had brought back fresh fruit, nothing like ever seen before on earth but that would look appetizing to the human eye if one were ever to gaze upon them.

Aurora rubbed her eyelids from sleeping all night and then ran up to the waterfall. She took off her garments, and the prince turned away immediately so as not to stare and be rude. Though he was a barbarian, he wasn't like the others whom those on earth were accustomed to. With time, barbarians had become more caring and intelligent. Aliya turned his head slowly to look at her from the most corner part of his eye. As each moment passed, he seemed to get more acquainted with her beauty and keener to converse with her to make her aware of his presence. At times, either through body language or thoughtful words, he would hint to her that he, in fact, was interested in her. A woman's intuition always was and still is above all, and our princess was well aware of the prince's feelings, for she felt the same way.

"Princess, please watch your surroundings. Jerreria has commanded I keep you safe," Aliya said as he grasped Zulkirnaan.

"Roarrr!" came the sound of Zulgini, who was nearby.

"Yes, how can I forget that you are tasked with the same duty, my dragon friend," Aliya said, standing tall and straight. He looked ahead for a second before turning his head to Aurora and smiling.

The princess could not help but smile back. Blood rushed to her cheeks, and she bashfully turned away just to look back and see if the prince was still gazing. An invisible bond between the two seemed to be forming, one that has formed between a male and a female since the beginning of time: the bond called love.

"I am the princess's guard and will protect her before any of you!" Gadlin said, meaning it.

"I can take care of myself!" Aurora said, "but I like that you are all here with me."

"Ride with me, princess?" Aliya said, not knowing how Aurora would react to his gesture. The princess finished getting ready and ran to him.

"Well, how can I say no to my hero!" she said, grabbing his hand and jumping onto Ragnor.

They began riding, and the prince was glad that she had accepted his request. They dashed through the forest, over the rivers and rocks. Gadlin would sometimes fall behind or go on ahead to scout with Zulgini, giving the prince and princess time to bond.

They told each other of their own land and how growing up was for them. Aurora told him about how she could heal with just her aura. She told him of the Forest of Angels and of her father, the king of the elves and that her favorite food was fairy cake and how she had always wanted to go on an adventure and that now she was finally getting to.

Aliya, never been able to be open with anyone, finally did so with an elven woman. His mother and father would probably disagree with their love, for Aurora wasn't of the barbarian kin, but these minuscule things no longer mattered to him. It didn't matter because he felt differently around her. He began to tell her of how he hunted and when he'd first met Ragnor, how he would live and travel in different parts of Arcadia alone so he could grow as a warrior.

He tried to explain his strange power that he could not control: when he turned into a berserker. Also, of the time he got Zulkirnaan by fighting the demon Kattz and defeating him at the lava rivers. An image of the day passed before his eyes: He stood on the huge body, holding the sword up after ripping it out of the demon's chest. The lava rivers surrounded them, clashing with one another and creating waves of fire. He had been in berserk mode, and the sword had felt his energy and chose him as its new wielder. In order for this to occur, the previous wielder had to be sacrificed by the new master.

Awakening from his daydream, Aliya quickly announced, "We are close to the Hidden Mist."

It was beyond the valley, a series of floating islands with little rocks floating around them. Some had trees or grass while others were plain. Some of the island's minerals or materials were different, giving them different colors, from crystal to ruby with shades of grey, black, and brown.

Zulgini landed next to Aliya and motioned the princess onto his back, for the rising path ahead was dangerous. She climbed off Ragnor, smiling and looking at the prince even as she then took off on the dragon. They had bonded, and she was feeling something she'd never felt before. It was love. She truly loved Aliya.

Meanwhile, in another part of Arcadia, an evil plan was brewing.

"I'm sending a wraith to help you," Abubak said through his black crystal ball to Usmak, who was riding his dragon.

"Tachakra will transform due to the wraith and the second moon being full. We shall attack then and take the princess for the ritual as planned. They make their way toward the Hidden Mist, where the fairy lives, but our guards are already in place."

No one knew that the princess was important to Dajjrah's plans. He still had not told the sorcerers what the ritual was for. Time was of the essence, and the time was coming near. He could not wait any longer. Banging his horns into the fire, he burned in pain and levitated back. Dajjrah could assume any form he wanted, but while encaged, he was in his true form: a goat for a head that resembled a bison's, with huge horns; human arms and chest, well defined like his abdomen, which was built to the core; and goat legs with huge black bat-like wings.

He was the end of all mankind and life in Arcadia as well as the whole universe.

CHAPTER 14

Queen Mermaid Elanor

Jerreria was not used to being alone on his journey, and he hoped Zulgini was all right without him. Though he was far more than capable of taking care of himself, best friends always worried about each other.

"Upward wind thrust!" he said, and a gust of wind came under his cloak and lifted him up into the air as if he were a giant flying squirrel. He flew over the hills, where a herd of dinosaurs and some Arcadian ground sloths—which were as big as polar bears—could be seen. As he passed over them, he dove down a waterfall that led into the Isle of Tantadoha. The Baiji flying dolphins danced and jumped at his sight as he sped past, gliding over them. He loved the water and all the creatures that lived above and within it. As he traveled along the isle, some polar bears stood on two feet, as if trying to grasp him. Tusked sea lions with manes blue in color were near the shore, lounging around and looking at our wizard as he flew by, causing the wake in the ocean to wash over them.

Such a hidden gem was the Isle of Tantadoha, an exotic Caribbean of Arcadia filled with aquatic wonders.

"Jerreria!" a group of mermaids yelled, waving their hands at him. He flew up and did a full flip before landing on a nearby rock that jutted out of the ocean.

"I must speak to Elanor at once," he said.

"What's the secret password for entry into Atlantia?"

"Could it be, 'In the water or sea, mermaids are fairest to see'?"

"Yes! Follow us!" they said as they laughed and plunged into the water.

Jerreria had his staff form an air bubble, which fit around his head like a helmet. He plunged into the water after them and swam as fast as he could because keeping up with mermaids underwater was no easy task. Huge creatures could be seen: aquatic dinosaurs, with big fins and elongated necks; a gigantic shark; and different exotic fish were also swimming past. The coral reef was lit with colors and lights of all sorts. It was heaven there; everything seemed as if in harmony.

As he went deeper into the ocean's abyss, a cavern full of life was coming into view. It was a city of mermaids, some men but most of them women. Mermaids ruled the underwater realm, and in the center of it all was Elanor's palace. Mermaids were able to come on shore for a short period but would die if they stay there for too long. Seldom did they come to land unless it was necessary.

Elanor lived in a palace that was dry so she would change back and forth from legs to fins when she deemed it necessary. When it came to meeting people from the land above the sea, she stayed in legged form to find common ground with land creatures.

Jerreria walked up the stairs that led out of the water and on toward the stairs that led into the mesmerizing palace. He always enjoyed a visit to the Sea Realm. It was relaxing and enjoyable at once. Elanor was a mermaid of great beauty and wisdom, for she had lived and ruled in Arcadia for quite some time. Her hair was white like a pearl, tied by blue and green seaweed. Her eyes were a mystical light blue and accommodated a powerful yet positive aura. Her fair skin gleamed of white sand and glittering water.

"Jerreria, I have been waiting for your arrival since I heard the news of Gora's passing. The evil one has infiltrated the land above. I felt a shift in your realm the day. Gora left us all. Now, sightings in the water of monsters and creatures not of our realm have been happening. It is time I tell you the whereabouts of the last two scrolls. Our scroll is no longer with us. The sea creature that carried it within its belly has been missing for two moons now. I personally would go visit it, the unicorn squid Uracraken.

"You must travel to the Island of Dragons and meet Father Dragon, for he has the last scroll in Arcadia. Tonight, stay with us, and we shall strategize together for my realm and yours. War comes from the Forest of Evil. It grows in evil Zusra and soon will open the doors to Dajjrah's minions and then to the evil one himself. All heavens and the universe are in danger of being engulfed in his eternal flame," Elanor said.

"I love your company, Elanor. You know that. Let us discuss other matters now, for your presence always helps soothe my mind, and lately things have been rather stressful," he said as she blushed at him, for no matter how old she was, something about Jerreria made her feel different every time she was with him. "I shall accompany you tonight and leave in the morning. I am a bit hungry from the swim. I would love to have some food from your realm, if possible, my dear."

"I shall have a feast prepared for you. Come, lie down and let me help you relax. Your Staff of Abazel, have you learned of its powers yet?" Elanor asked.

"Well, I haven't had the chance yet and do not know where to start," Jerreria answered.

"I shall help you talk to Gora. You must reach out to your mentor to understand its true nature."

She beckoned him into a bed of water, shaped like a huge clamshell, glowing aquatic light blue. The water had healing properties and could also charge one's telepathic ability to communicate with the Arcadian space-time continuum, where Gora's consciousness was now residing. Jerreria closed his eyes and rested his head back until it was submerged in the semiviscous liquid. First, everything went dark then all he could see were spots of illuminations that began to converge.

CHAPTER 15

⟋ ⟨ ⟩ ⟍

Gora the Galient's Advice

Jerreria awoke in a realm of light. Across the way, he saw a figure seated with his back slightly turned, as if he had been awaiting Jerreria's arrival in this new place. He took a step forward, and it felt like he was walking on water, and clouds were emerging from it, passing through, up, and down, creating hills of mist all around him. He started to glide toward the figure, almost as though he was skating on ice.

"Hello, Jerreria. It has been quite some time since we last met," Gora said, chuckling. "Tell me, what's new in Arcadia?"

"Well, Sir, I have been having premonitions, and I have assembled a team," Jerreria answered.

"Yes, I know of your forthcomings, as I have been watching you through the ripples of time. The prince and princess sure have grown. Even now, they make their way through the Hidden Mist. Let me show you." He pointed with his staff toward the water.

In the water, Jerreria saw Aurora flying atop Zulgini and the other two climbing up the floating hills and rocks of the Hidden Mist. He missed his companions and couldn't wait to be with them again.

"Gora, I need your help comprehending the Staff of Abazel. Its powers, I do not understand yet. If I could just learn how to use it, I'm sure I could save Arcadia."

"Why yes, my young apprentice. This staff in your possession is indeed powerful. It's said that the One, our Creator, had his angels forge it themselves. It contains power of time and space. But the limits of its powers depend on its wielder. You must train yourself in this realm to be able to use it in Arcadia. Let's start by slowing time so that, as we practice here, time will pass slowly in Arcadia, and you will return with some newfound skills."

"And how do I do that, Gora?" Jerreria asked eagerly.

"Begin by focusing on the two crystals on top of your staff, and use your aura to make them spin in rotation. The crystals use the energy around them as a power source that reaches into the very atoms of the matter around you. Once they are activated, take yourself to the Fountain of Life. Under its mystical waterfall, gather your aura. Think the thought of revelation. One of pure blood can slow time. Maybe even travel in it," Gora explained.

Jerreria closed his eyes and concentrated. The crystals separated themselves from the main crystal on the staff and began rotating slowly then with more speed. He created another Jerreria in Arcadia under the waterfall, who was thinking the thought of slowing time. As he did so, the flow of water began to slow. A nearby forest fly and an Ora Nak's fairy's wings did as well while they moved as fast as a hummingbird's in our world.

"Good!" Gora said. "Now, let us begin. First, you shall learn to fight with the crystal staff."

As both got into their fighting stances, they used similar moves as monks do on our planet but with a magical spin.

"Each staff is different, and the way you fight with it is different too. You must be one with the staff. Your soul must be attuned to it," Gora said as he struck with a combo of quick attacks. Then another Gora formed behind him and also attacked Jerreria, overwhelming him. Jerreria began fighting both Goras, displaying a series of flips and acrobatic moves while guarding each of his mentor's attacks.

"Your defense is good as usual, but can you attack and connect with your opponents? They take power from the Zusra, a powerful source of dark magic. You must learn your new powers to take them on and yet survive, my young boy!" Gora told his apprentice.

Every attack was stronger and harder until Jerreria reached a point of frustration and a white energy began to form at the tip of the crystal. It seemed that in times of great stress, the crystal reacted to Jerreria and would build up pure aura energy and emit a cosmic blast. In this case, it took out both Goras, causing the false one to disappear.

"Well done!" Gora remarked. "Now, let's try six of me," he said as they surrounded Jerreria. This was going to be a long day or hour or minute—depending on where in the realm you were located.

CHAPTER 16

Fairy of the Mist

It was a magnificent journey on which to spectate, as the prince made his way up the Islands of the Hidden Mist. At first, Ragnor leaped from rock to rock, exhibiting excellent agility. Aurora was surveying the area with Zulgini from above. As the cliffs got farther apart and harder to climb, there came a point where Gadlin had to stay behind, for he was unable to keep up with the others.

"Don't worry about me. I shall await your arrival here and make camp with my steed," Gadlin said as the dragon circled to make sure that his companion was okay.

Aliya was on a floating rock ahead of the island Gadlin had stopped on and told Ragnor to stay back with them and guard the camp. The horse's ability to make it that far had impressed him, but it was an elven stallion, and elven horses were far stronger than the average ones on Earth.

"Gadlin, lend me your elven ropes," Aliya said to his new friend.

"Why, of course, prince," he replied as he tossed it to him.

Aliya took the rope and tied it to the end of Zulkirnaan. He began spinning the large sword and threw it with all his might toward the island nearest to him. He was rocketed forward with the sword, almost as if he flew across the open sky. Barbarians were strong men who did not fear death, and Aliya was proving that to his friends as they watched him move from one floating rock to another, stabbing his sword into the side of the island as if it were his enemy.

Once he made it to the halfway mark, he stopped with the princess and Zulgini for some food. The princess prepared an elven meal that satisfied his stomach and heart. The view of Arcadia was amazing, for all Arcadia was seen from such heights. They sat under a dragon tree and pointed out all the different parts they recognized until their eyes fell on the Evil Forest. At once, they realized that Arcadia was indeed in dire need of their help, for the evil Zusra could be seen taking over, its dark magic destroying every life source as it spread.

"Let us collect our fairy and hasten on our journey, for I sense that the evil is more apparent than ever, Aliya. Ride with me to the top. It is but a few islands away," Aurora told the prince.

Aliya had never been on a dragon and was nervous to try so. Zulgini also never let anyone but Jerreria ride him, and he was allowing other creations to do so, though his pride told him not to. It was a time when new alliances and strategies had to be implemented, for all the universe was at the disposal of the Zusra. Zulgini lowered his wing, and Aliya climbed on and took a seat behind the princess. The dragon jumped off the edge of the cliff they were on and headed to the top and final island, where the fairy was known to hide.

They neared the top of the island and discovered that it wasn't as big as they had anticipated. Zulgini flew in close and both leaped off his back and onto the little oasis.

Jagged cliffs dressed the rest of the island, as if to protect it from trespassers. The area was too small for him to land, so he dropped them off and flew down to check on the rest of their companions.

"Hello, Fairy of the Mist. It is I, Princess Aurora, here with Prince Aliya, on behalf of Jerreria. We need your services on our journey to find the lost scrolls. All Arcadia calls upon you to help."

"And why sacrifice my well-being for creatures that have never noticed or cared for me?" a tiny voice, its whereabouts still unknown to them, asked.

"I am Aliya of Barbaria," the prince began. "I have seen the land and the monsters that are now in Arcadia, and I can say that it won't be long 'till the Hidden Mist and all its creatures and fairies are infected by this evil Zusra that spreads."

"How do I know you do not serve the evil one himself? A test of bravery, let us call it," the tiny voice challenged them.

With that said, two stone Minotaurs—one with a sword and shield and the other carrying a huge ax—came to life.

"Only the true of heart will be able to stop my stone guardians." As she finished her sentence, the battle began.

Surprising as it may have seemed, Aurora ran first, catching Aliya off guard. She jumped into the air and formed her bow of enchantment. It materialized in her hands as she pulled an arrow of light from her quiver. She shot at the Minotaur with the ax first, but it deflected her arrow. She kept running at him, taking out her small elven sword from the sheath on the waist of her back, striking the huge beast as she moved past him with speed and agility. Aliya, on the other hand, was going blow for blow with the sword-wielding one. Zulkirnaan and the Minotaur's swords collided, sending sparks as they did so.

The Minotaur was strong, but Aliya was still able to keep up with him. He swung his sword, spinning as he thrust it, using the weight of the sword, and the spinning motions to create a blender-like attack. The beast used his shield to block it and then hit Aliya with such force that he went flying into a nearby tree, breaking it on contact.

"Aliya, are you all right?" Aurora asked as she continued to dodge her enemy's ax.

There was no reply, so she ran toward him but was blocked by a huge shield. A large bull-like hand grabbed Aurora and lifted her off the ground. She began to yell, "Let me go, you wretched beast!"

Just then, a sword came flying, spinning at a hundred miles per hour. Such force and accuracy at that moment to save his love's life. In the light, a sheen from the rope connected to the blade was seen, and at that very moment, it struck. It cut off the giant beast's hand and head, turning him into stone once again. Aliya caught the princess in midair and the head and hand he had chopped off from the Minotaur crashed into the ground and shattered into thousands of pieces. He swung the rope and aimed it at the other monster, who deflected it with his ax. Angry at his brother's death, the standing beast took his brother's sword and threw his ax, which severed Zulkirnaan from the elven rope. Zulkirnaan went flying, landing in the earth and out of our hero's reach.

"Princess, use your enchanted bow to distract him as I get my sword and end his days in Arcadia," Aliya told Aurora.

"Yes, let us conquer him together!" Aurora concurred.

They ran on either side of him, making their way toward Zulkirnaan, who was placed directly behind the beast. Aurora formed the bow and shot a couple of arrows toward his eyes, blocking his vision as Aliya slid past him and grabbed his sword. At that moment, the prince quickly took it and dragged it behind him, running toward the beast. The Minotaur also began running at him and, in a flash, they collided.

But Zulkirnaan was too powerful. A large split began to turn the beast into stone as Aliya landed behind him in a crouched position. The beast fell into two halves, shattering into many small pieces. They had defeated the guardians of the fairy.

"Ifritis, Bullenidus!" A fairy flew out of a nearby tree. "I can't believe you defeated my guardians! Who is the brave soul that did so?"

"Well, it was us," Aurora said as the fairy, who was only five inches in height, flew up to the prince and hugged his ear.

"Oh, my prince! You have saved me! I wasn't allowed to leave the Hidden Mist and have been trapped here by the evil sorcerers. They left the beasts to stop anyone from freeing me. You have saved my fairy life, and I shall go with you on your journey!" the small creature said as she flew, dropping a wake of fairy dust.

She was beautiful, with small fairy wings that glowed like neon lights, pink and blue. Her hair was short and black while her skin was tan and her smile to die for. She had huge hazel eyes that could see right through you. If she had been of human size, it would have been hard for our prince to decide which beauty to give his heart to. Aliya smirked at the thought of having a fairy companion on this adventure. He'd always had a way with women; they all loved our prince not only for his good looks and masculine body, but for his ability to look death in the face without flinching.

They began to talk when a loud crash was heard from below. They looked over the edge and saw that all hell had broken loose.

CHAPTER 17

Surprise Attack

Zulgini yelled in pain as the wraith attacked him. Wraiths were huge masses of blood-orange Zusra, manifested from sacrificing and entrapping an innocent soul. Only its eyes could be seen through the black smoky mist that created a cloak and warlock-like hat, pointy at the very tip. It was as big as a dragon and it flew leaving Zusra energy in the atmosphere like chemtrails. It shot electricity at Zulgini, and at that moment, from both of its sides, little black imps began to come forth out of the mysterious portals that appeared from nowhere.

It was a link to the Evil Forest. They started bringing minions from the lower realms into Arcadia. Usmak smiled as his tongue came out to taste the fear in the air. He hovered on his dragon at a distance, watching as the imps flew in by the horde. Their plan was being executed perfectly. Soon, the princess would be at their disposal.

Zulgini yelled in his head, *"Jerreria, we need you here! Everyone is in danger!"*

He continued to fly around and fight the wraith as it attacked him. He blew his starlike fire onto the evil entity. The creature hissed in dismay, getting angrier, for it was a flame of purity that burned like no other.

Gadlin and Ragnor, bombarded by the imps, began to fight them. Gadlin formed the enchanted bow and shot one imp, then two, then three. An excellent marksman, he never wasted an arrow. Ragnor tore the imps from the sky, ripping off their wings and limbs and roaring in might.

Imps were nasty creatures, ruled by their master, RukRuk, the much larger imp, the first of the imp kind. The imp's wings were like bats', and their skin pitch-black. They had a red glow in their dark eyes, as if they were filled with blood. They grinned with large sharp teeth, many of them stretching from pointy ear to pointy ear. They had three fingers and one thumb, with large hooklike claws. They loved feeding on aura or soul energy from the living. It was like a drug that they could not resist. Imps loved living in mountains and caves and usually came out at night to feed. Now, evil was showing itself in the day, for darkness was spreading its reaches farther than ever before.

RukRuk was there on a special mission: to capture the princess. He barely fit through the portal due to his size. All he said was "RukRuk" and the rest was telepathic.

"RukRuk," he said as he flew around, looking for the princess. The imps were many and had all our friends occupied.

Though fairies were small, their strength was immensely greater than one might think. Aliya landed on the island next to Ragnor and Gadlin, with the princess and our fairy. The fairy began protecting the prince and princess from nearby imps as Aurora formed her bow and began taking them out of the sky. Aliya, swinging Zulkirnaan in all directions, was also taking out all the imps that crossed his path. Usmak landed on the island next to them, on the other side. Aliya, not waiting for anyone, threw Zulkirnaan, which he had reunited with the elven rope, to meet the sorcerer.

"Who is thisss?" Usmak asked as he formed two swords from the evil Zusra.

"I am your end, creature!" Aliya said as he sprinted toward him to attack but was met with the flame of Usmak's dragon. He used Zulkirnaan to block it, kneeling behind the massive weapon while it lit up, glowing red, as if he was in berserker mode. Just then, Zulgini swooped in and grabbed the dragon, pulling it with him off the floating island. The wraith behind them flew past Usmak and Aliya as they fought each other. Both were showboating their impressive techniques and acrobatics, one strike after another, barely missing but tearing apart the terrain around them.

"You are no match for me, barbarian!" Usmak shrieked, as he froze him in midtrack with his red Zusra cobra. "RukRuk, grab the princesss!" the sorcerer hissed as his snake hood opened in anger.

"RukRuk," RukRuk said, as he began closing in on her. All our heroes at that moment jumped closer to the princess to protect her. Gadlin pulled out his sword and combined it with his bow to form an enchanted crossbow. He unleashed light arrows like a machine gun, fighting off imps that were closing in on them.

"Protect the princess!" Aliya yelled in despair. Then, out of nowhere, flew in the fairy, causing Usmak to lose concentration. Aliya, free from the Zusra, grabbed his sword and jumped toward the other island, only fearing for the princess and not for his own life. He realized that, at that very moment, he had finally found someone worthy of loving.

Meanwhile, Tachakra, jumping from island to island, made his way toward the battle, ready for his revenge. He wanted to kill the man who had annihilated his whole pack. The evil Zusra running in his aura made his anger wilder than before. The wraith, sensing the wolf, started to spread like a dark cloud until the whole sky was engulfed. Tachakra landed on the island where the princess was located at the same time as Aliya. He began to transform into his saber wolf form. The battle had just begun.

CHAPTER 18

Saber Wolf

The darkness seemed to give strength to all the creatures of evil, as the imps were taking more arrows than before. Aliya, knowing his friends did not stand a chance against Tachakra, he ran at the saber wolf with Zulkirnaan raised high in both hands to draw his focus away from the others. Ragnor came running to help but was knocked away with one swipe of Tachakra's hand. Tachakra snarled in anger at Aliya as he lunged forward at his target. Both began throwing blows at each other, claws and sword swinging furiously and creating large gashes in both their armor and their bodies. Aliya swung his sword low, trying to knock him down by tripping the wolf. Maybe, if he was lucky, he would cut off both legs. Tachakra jumped and connected with a punch to Aliya's back, sending him hurtling to the ground. He got up, knocking the dust off himself and smiling. He loved battles and lived for this very moment. He took the elven rope that was wrapped around his right arm and loosened it so that he could swing his sword. He created momentum and sent it flying toward Tachakra, who jumped once again, but this time, though he dodged Zulkirnaan, he was met with Aliya's fist, which connected to him with full force. He went flying ten feet in the air and landed a distance away. He stood up and fell to his knees again for a second, shaking his head. Aliya was keeping up with the saber wolf now and, with each battle, was becoming a stronger warrior.

While our heroes fought on the island for their dear lives, Zulgini and Kraynick fought in the sky. Zulgini, trying his best to burn imps out of the sky to help his friends, also had to make sure he drew Kraynick's red flame away from them. The Hidden Mist was being destroyed. Such beauty was burned within minutes of rampaging battle.

Usmak began chanting in his demonic language, and vampire orcs started to appear, pulling themselves out of the ground.

"Usmak, you will never change. Up to no good, as usual," a familiar voice said.

"Jerreria, you finally have joined us. I have been waiting for you." He turned to see our wizard floating in midair twenty feet from him. Something had changed in Jerreria, and Usmak could sense it.

"Why do you attack my companions?" the wizard asked in anger.

"Why do we do the things we do?" Usmak asked in return. "Because it serves our purpossse! Why else!" he said as he sent his Zusra snake spiraling at Jerreria.

"Ssss!" Usmak yelled, but as his snake passed through Jerreria, the real one reappeared above him.

"Staff of Abazel!" he yelled. As the light emitted, it stopped Usmak's Zusra cobra while penetrating the darkness of the wraith. The wraith, unable to handle such energy, turned back into its original form and began fleeing in pain. Everyone stopped to look up, and after the light started clearing, they recognized their friend Jerreria! It gave everyone a sense of hope, and they began taking down the enemies together as a unit.

Zulgini flew in, and Jerreria threw him a flask of the Fountain of Life's water, which he swallowed in one gulp and immediately felt the effects of. He did a full flip and came up behind Kraynick, burning him out of the sky with this new flame that he got from the water. It burned brightly, and Kraynick turned to dust, who was unable to handle the fire from Zulgini's mouth.

Usmak yelled in anger and attacked Jerreria. Forming his Zusra swords, he fought him in midair. Usmak could tell that he could not keep up with Jerreria's newfound strength. Jerreria fought him with ease, waiting for each of his attacks and perfectly countering them. It was as if he knew exactly what move Usmak was going to make next. How was he able to overpower the evil Zusra given to him by Lord Dajjrah? It made Usmak even angrier. He opened his hood and yelled in frustration, but he knew this battle was over.

"Grab the princess, RukRuk!" he yelled as he disappeared into a portal.

Meanwhile, Aliya, still fighting Tachakra on one side of the island to keep the beast away from his companions, noticed the wolf returning to his original form since the wraith had left, and he took advantage of that moment. With a single blow from the bottom of the handle on his sword, he knocked the lycan out.

RukRuk, flying to the other end of the island, was met by Ragnor and Gadlin, who were protecting the princess. As RukRuk came in, Ragnor bit his leg and hung on as Gadlin pushed Aurora out of the way and took her place in the clutches of the evil minion.

RukRuk, thinking he had caught the princess, flew right into a portal that led into the Evil Forest, but with Ragnor at his leg and Gadlin in his arm. The two royal guardians had been captured, and all the warriors could do was watch in agony.

"Gadlin, no!" the princess yelled, running to the edge of the island. Aliya was close behind because Ragnor had been taken through the portal as well. Both Aliya and Aurora had just lost a loved one, someone they had known since birth.

CHAPTER 19

Naveen

Everyone at camp was passing around the last of the water from the Fountain of Life as it healed their wounds. It had been a tremendous battle for both sides. Although Usmak's dragon had been burnt out of the sky by Zulgini, they had lost the princess's guardian as well as the prince's lion.

Jerreria sat and smoked from his pipe, something he did often when puzzled. Why did they want the princess instead of the last two scrolls? It was a question that was really bothering him, for he knew nothing good was to come of it. Tachakra had been captured and detained by elven ropes that could not be broken by strength, for it was enchanted by Jerreria himself.

"The beast will lead us to our friends!" Aliya said, looking at Tachakra from across the fire.

"I must meditate on the Mushramushrooms. Watch our new guest, Zulgini," he said as he got up and searched for a place nearby.

He searched through the Arcadian library until he came to the scroll of prophecy. In it, he read that it was necessary to have a virgin of royal blood who would help open the fire cage where the evil lord was trapped in. He saw Aurora yelling, chained to two huge Roman-like pillars. Then a portal in front of her opened and Zusra began flowing through her body and into the portal. He saw the eyes first, then the head, and then the fire as it extinguished his foresight. He had just had his first encounter with Dajjrah, and he felt the evil that he was. He saw how the Zusra would spread first in Arcadia then into the heavens and universe, infecting every living creature. Only the scrolls could save them, and it was necessary that they found the last two. Afraid to tell the princess why they wanted her, he told Zulgini first telepathically, and then, as he returned to camp to tell the others, he was greeted by an unexpected surprise.

"Is this Jerreria whom I have heard so much about?" the fairy asked, flying up to his face, grabbing his beard, then his hat, and looking under it. "He doesn't seem so special to me like Prince Aliya," she said, leaving a trail of fairy dust as she flew around him, a look of confusion on her face.

"And who might this little thing be?" Jerreria asked, though he knew it was the fairy he had summoned.

"I am Naveen, the Fairy of the Hidden Mist. Your brave prince and princess freed me from the sorcerer's monsters and asked for me to join the quest for the lost scrolls."

"What do you say to that, my little fairy friend? Arcadia needs someone with your abilities. I saw you in one of my visions and asked them to go and get you."

"I waited for this all my life! I was told that one day a man with a staff of the first wizard would ask me to join his adventure and that I was to accompany him through the trials that lay ahead, as well as protecting the prince and princess. When I saw they had arrived, I was thrilled, for I had been waiting for a century or more," Naveen said.

Jerreria smirked. "We must head to the Island of Dragons, and along the way, Aliya, you must meet Hamza, the saber-toothed tiger. Only he can carry you and Zulkirnaan on this journey."

Aliya looked away, missing his best friend and worrying about what was to become of him. They all rested around the fire on fur blankets. No one wanted to sleep alone in the tents, especially the princess. It had been quite a day for everyone, and it wasn't going to get any easier. Tachakra sat and looked at this group that intrigued him. Especially the wizard. He could have disposed of him hours ago, but they had shown mercy. It was a trait he was not familiar with.

"Tachakra, would you like some fairy cake?" Aurora asked, catching him off guard.

She put it forward toward his mouth as he turned his face away. Fairy food for a wolf? He wasn't used to such things, but hunger was setting in. "I will leave it here for you. Don't be such a werewolf." And she placed the steaming hot cake next to him. He watched as she returned to her seat. It was the first time someone had shown kindness to him. This group was different indeed. Maybe he was the one who was wrong, or at least the thought was beginning to make its way into his head.

CHAPTER 20

~つ♀ᡕ~

The Hydra

They traveled through the passes, mountains, rivers, and hills until they saw the Crystal Castle. From there, they met with Hamza, who was notified by Gora to meet them along the way. To gain Hamza's trust, Aliya was asked to wrestle him almost to the death. He almost lost before Jerreria yelled at Hamza that he was just a young lad. Hamza, still surprised by the barbarian's strength, allowed him to ride on his back. This was a true honor for any barbarian, for Hamza was the king of all beasts. Hamza was much larger than the lions in Barbaria, and he was also much stronger than them. These attributes made him a perfect fit for carrying Zulkirnaan, the mystical sword of fire. Our prince mounted his new companion, and they both dashed ahead as if trying to get a feel for each other. Zulgini, from the sky, had a hard time keeping up with Hamza, for he was one of Arcadia's fastest creatures.

In the Evil Forest, Abubak was walking alongside the rotting trees. The ground around him was cracking open with evil Zusra pouring through it. The whole forest was almost consumed by evil, spreading a sort of barrier through the surrounding areas. The vampire orcs were eating animals and attacking nearby homes and villages. They had herded the different dinosaurs and were using them as steeds. Some were found on T. rexes, and some on large raptors with jagged teeth. Others rode on the ones with shields for heads, adding armor to their bodies and giving them a medieval appearance. Now, evil was openly making its way into the realm, and Abubak was at the heart of it.

Isra and Usmak were also creating their own minions. Usmak was taking all the reptiles and, with his Zusra, transforming them into his servants. Isra was turning people into different monsters or orcs—whatever the Zusra made of them. Some became channels for other beings from other realms, taking over their physical bodies. Others transferred themselves into the realm, exchanging the soul of an innocent in order for them to materialize in Arcadia. An army full of trolls, vampire orcs, imps, wraiths, reptilians, and jinn were being formed, and they all had one mission: find the final two scrolls and retrieve the princess.

Jerreria had trained all his companions through rounds of meditation. Aliya surprised him with his strength and ability to wield his mystic blade. One incident occurred during their session that worried Jerreria though. The demon within Aliya was attempting to fuse with his soul; it spoke out to Jerreria's consciousness. Kattz told him the prince would one day call upon him for help, and that day, the demon would return.

Jerreria awoke that night from meditation with chills because the thought that one day Aliya would give in to Kattz's will provoked dread in him. When it came to Tachakra, it was more like therapy. He had one-on-one conversations with his subconscious while everyone slept.

As they traveled, he noticed that Tachakra began to understand the power of aura. The princess would pray over him, and now it felt good to the wolf. He was released of his restraints and began journeying with them as a member rather than an enemy. He told them what he knew of the sorcerers' plans and asked the princess for forgiveness after all the kindness she had shown him. He had found his new pack and understood that what he'd been doing before was wrong. Jerreria had already seen him in a dream but had never made it evident for fear of what the others would say. He knew that he would play an important role in their quest, though Tachakra didn't know it himself.

They finally arrived at the Isle of Tantadoha. The Island of Dragons was just over the horizon and couldn't be seen from the coast, where it seemed as if all life had left it. What was going on? Where had the life gone? Why was the water so still?

Then, out of the water came a nine-headed beast. It was not of this world and must have been the reason all the mermaids were nowhere to be found. It was time to take on the sea creature. It stood between them and Father Dragon, holder of one of the last ancient scrolls.

CHAPTER 21

Wizard's End

Reaching into the clouds, the Hydra was huge, bigger than Father Dragon himself. The heads resembled a dragon's, but the ears were finlike. Each head had a mind of its own, and if one head was cut off, two more emerged in its place. The Hydra towered over everyone and began shooting poisonous gas that infected everything in the vicinity.

In the water, a school of flying dolphins emerged. On one of their backs was Elanor, the queen mermaid. On her tail were Qalupaliks, transformed mermaids from the evil Zusra emitted by the Hydra. They looked evil, with sharp teeth and dilated black eyes. Their skin was a slimy green, almost of decay. They also had long black hair, and no noses were to be seen. They were like witches in the water, feeding off the aura of animals and humanoids. They loved children and sought them out as delicacies.

"Look, Jerreria, it's a mermaid!" Naveen pointed out, surprised to see one for the first time.

"Quickly, Zulgini. Stop these creatures from attacking her!" Jerreria told his dragon.

The dragon flew toward the mermaid but was attacked by the head of the Hydra nearest him. Aliya, in an attempt to help his friend, began to spin until he let go of Zulkirnaan that flew through the sky like a frisbee on fire. It cut off the head of the Hydra that was attacking Zulgini, but as the head plunged into the water, two more emerged. Everyone was stunned by what they saw. Then together, they started to attack. The princess ran along the cliffside, first shooting her enchanted arrows at the beast then at some of the nearby Qalupaliks. Zulgini, barely getting away from the Hydra's attack, burned the evil creatures that followed the mermaid queen.

"Zulgini, take me to the top, high above the beast. Tachakra and Aliya, keep the enemy's attacks from behind at bay," Jerreria instructed.

They both turned around to see hordes of attacking orcs. The invasion was in full effect. This was the forefront, before the Island of Dragons, and it needed to be protected at all costs. Aliya looked at Tachakra, who smirked for the first time. It was time he proved himself to his new friends. His mouth open and claws out, he lunged forward. Aliya was right beside him, his sword raised to the sky, but Hamza was first to attack. Jumping above them and taking the first vampire orc atop a shield-headed dinosaur, he used his huge fangs and jaws to separate the creature's body from its head. They began battling—barbarian, lycan, and sabretooth—going back and forth as if in a competition. Hamza was tearing orcs limb from limb as he pounced on one creature to the next while Aliya and Tachakra sliced through the horde of evil creatures. Though they were fewer in number compared to the army of evil, the army could not withstand our warriors.

Zulgini, at the top, saw a figure standing on the Hydra's tallest head. It was Abubak. This must have been his dragon, transformed from his evil Zusra. Zulgini flew up to the sorcerer and hovered so that Jerreria could have a conversation with him. The beast's head which Abubak stood on was almost as big as Zulgini's body, truly a monster to be reckoned with.

"Your master was weak, and so are you, Jerreria!" Abubak said, and a storm formed above him.

"Gora loved you like a son. How could you betray him? Wasn't he a father to you, Abubak? Look at yourself! Look at what you have become! You are overcome with the evil Zusra. Come to the light while you still can, or your soul will be doomed for an eternity," Jerreria pleaded with his senior wizard.

Jerreria began reminiscing about when he and Abubak had competed as young children. Abubak, older and taller than our young hero, always tried to use Jerreria to show off to the rest of their class—the experiments in Magic Chemistry with horned toads, where he pranked Jerreria's to explode; or in Metaphysics Magic, when they would battle on the crystal balcony of the huge Crystal Castle. He remembered one instance in particular, when Abubak had almost killed him during practice.

They gathered their aura as light particles swirled around them and then attacked each other just as they were about to do now. Though much older, their rivalry remained. The only difference from back then was that Jerreria was no longer going to hold back. Lightning crackled above them as both gathered their power. Abubak, unaware of Jerreria's new training, didn't realize that he had gained more power than he had during their first altercation.

Jerreria grabbed the last of the Mushramushrooms and chanted a light growing spell directed at them. He telepathically told Zulgini to eat them and then lunged forward with his crystal staff, attacking Abubak. Zulgini grew and grew and grew until he was as big as the Hydra.

Then it was as if two titans were about to battle. Zulgini, grabbing the Hydra by three of its heads, blew his flame, completely burning them off before six grew back in their place. As the two dragons fought, our wizards displayed quite the battle themselves. A mixture of sword action with their staves, to kicks and punches, had one wizard countering the other's moves.

Jerreria seemed to be pushing Abubak farther and farther down the Hydra's neck until the two were jumping and clashing in midair. Jerreria was glowing in pure aura, white and blue like moonlight. Abubak was infused with a maroon, demonic-purple Zusra.

"Jerreria, I can burn his beast to hell if I go full force, but you must get out of the way, or you will also be killed," Zulgini said as he and the beast clawed at each other.

Then the Hydra grabbed him, and all the heads began to charge up, as if to attack Zulgini. With that many heads, not only would Zulgini die, but everyone battling in the area would, too, for the blast radius would totally annihilate everything, much like a nuclear warhead. The Hydra unleashed its attack, and at that very instant, a flash of lightning from where Jerreria was located occurred.

Jerreria remembered all the times he and Zulgini had fun flying, eating, and even sleeping by the campfire, the two of them jetting through the clouds and battling different monsters. He wouldn't let Zulgini—or any of his friends—get hurt. The fire from the Hydra's heads seemed to be getting sucked into something. Jerreria appeared in front of it the instant before contact and used his staff to bend light, space, and time to create a mini light hole (similar to a black hole in space) that absorbed the evil Zusra and the ensuing attack. In anger, the Hydra spread out all its heads, reaching different angles and heights, to throw our heroes off their next attacks. Abubak must have told the Hydra to change its strategy, for beasts like that didn't have the ability to make such immediate strategic changes. Jerreria used the Staff of Abazel to create multiple Jerrerias that blocked the Hydra's attacks, deflecting their flames while protecting his dragon.

His original waited in the center of the battle, as if in a meditative state. He opened his eyes at once, and in his mind yelled, "Zulgini, now! Attack with everything you have!" Jerreria teleported onto his dragon's head and let go of his crystal staff as it spun furiously in front of him as if to amplify his next attack. He put his hands together, and electricity began to form in a ball that grew in size. He and Zulgini, together, let go of their blast, Zulgini's star flame and Jerreria's aura blasting through it. The Hydra and Abubak disappeared in the flame, as if each and every one of their atoms were simultaneously exploding on contact.

On the cliffs of the isle, Tachakra and Aliya fought orcs, one after another. Naveen helped by blinding them and throwing them off their monsters. Naveen wanted to protect the prince, so she flew up and blinded one of the T. rexes, as it was about to bite Aliya from behind. It stepped onto one of the orcs and fell to the ground, as our fairy flew right through its eyeball and out of the other eye. Surrounded by many, Aliya swung his sword with the elven rope and threw it around the leg of one of the dinosaurs. They were huge, long necked brachiosauruses. They had duck-like faces and were taller than any tree in our world. Gray, scaly armor protected the creature; it had four pillars for legs.

A number of orcs were perched on top of it in tents, shooting arrows of fire from above. Aliya pulled with all his strength, but it wasn't enough to trip the large beast. Then, without warning, Tachakra came over and helped pull as hard as he could. Together, our heroes got the large beast to fall, creating a domino effect and taking two more with them.

Hamza, on the other side with Aurora, was making sure the princess was okay, as she sometimes shot two or even three arrows at once. She did spectacular flips, releasing arrows from every angle, and taking many orcs with her. She landed atop Hamza and told him to run by the other two dinosaurs that housed the archer vampire orcs atop them. She jumped off Hamza, who gave her a boost with his back. In midair, she threw her sword in the eye of one as she shot arrows at the other. The creatures fell atop one another, taking out the monstrous soldiers below.

From behind came Elanor on her flying dolphin, throwing spears of water-shaped tridents. The rumor was that she was the daughter of the sea king Poseidon. Her strength was great enough to crack the earth with one swipe of her spear. Behold, her warrior mermaids in leg form! They were on polar bears in pearl armor, riding for war and holding different sea weapons. Water swords were the main ones. As they came to help, Jerreria swooped in with Zulgini, the effects of the Mushramushrooms now worn off. Jerreria landed next to Elanor and told her it was necessary that her forces hold off the monsters as they made their way to the Island of Dragons to get one of the lost scrolls. She told him they would die trying and yelled, "For Arcadia!" She summoned a huge blue whale named Bahamut, which was much larger than the blue whales in our world. It had six fins, three on each side. Jerreria told everyone to jump onto the creature from above the isle as he made his way with Zulgini.

The final battle awaited, for the Island of Dragons was already under attack.

CHAPTER 22

Island of Dragons

Aurora held tight to Hamza and the prince as they rode onto the land. The island was a beautiful site: It was filled with huge prehistoric waterfalls, tropical and wondrous fruits hanging from exotic trees, and different ferns with exotic flowers shaped like stars were simultaneously changing color and size.

Jerreria flew in and saw that orcs on pterodactyls were flying in and attacking all the dragons to whom the island was home. In addition, the large wraith was taking over the body of different dragons, much like an evil entity would, by jumping from one dragon to another. He would make them attack, burning one another out of the sky. Isra's dragon had been transformed into a flying serpent; it was miles in length and sparkled like the ocean. Its scales were fishlike and as strong as the toughest metal on earth. Its head had whiskers that stretched across its beak-like face. It looked as though it belonged in the ocean and not the sky. Jerreria needed to make sure Father Dragon was okay, but how could he with such chaos around him?

"Don't worry, Jerreria. I shall protect you as you glide. Make your way to Father. Only you can help him if he is in danger. I will catch up after I help my brothers out," Zulgini said.

Jerreria dived forward through the sky battle as Zulgini blasted a few orcs out of the way of his master as he passed them.

On the ground, Aliya rode up to one of the giants and the princess jumped off, climbing up the beast as if she were a gymnast or acrobat. Princess Aurora's agility was of the highest caliber among all women in her forest. She lifted her sword and decapitated the giant then jumped toward the next one. In the jungle, Tachakra was hunting different trolls, as they destroyed everything around them by creating fires and harming the forest and the life within. The wolf would not stand for it. He attacked with all his might, but it seemed almost impossible for our heroes that day, for the enemy was many, and they were but a few.

Zulgini began to fight Isra's serpent, a dragon leviathan named Serebus that shot ice fire and froze everything it touched. Dark blue in color with aquatic blue scales for an underbelly, it flew through the sky as if it were underwater.

Somewhat resembling a Chinese dragon in shape, its face was pointy with a snout like a bird's or reptilian swordfish's. As it flew, the nearby clouds froze. Its touch was death itself, for its rider, Isra, was now our world's greeter of death. He had already hurt Father Dragon, but now, Isra commanded him to kill Zulgini instead, for he knew that Zulgini posed a major threat to their plans. Isra also sent a command to the orcs flying on the dinosaurs to jump onto Zulgini while he and Serebus distracted him. They flanked to the side, and Isra motioned for them to attack Zulgini from above. They stuck their weapons into the dragon as he did a three-sixty, shaking them off. They had injured his wing, making it difficult for him to fly.

Aliya looked up and told Naveen to protect the princess. She listened to her prince, for she had given her heart to him. She flew past some orcs, taking their weapons and making them use them on the surrounding orcs, for her strength was yet more than they could handle. The princess was fighting, but it was getting harder and harder for her to keep up with everyone else until one of the orcs struck her on the head with a sledgehammer. She was tired and could no longer keep up in battle. The orcs seized the moment and grabbed her. They started making their way up the mountain path when Aliya saw them taking her away. He became enraged and shifted right into berserk mode. The enemy was not ready for what was going to happen next.

Aliya ran, cutting the giant's Achilles' heel nearest to him. He then jumped up to his back to drag his sword down his spine, ripping it in half. The island was getting more infested with monsters, but it didn't matter. He killed a troll and then took out four orcs in a single swing. It was a massacre, the way Aliya was moving through the enemy; he briefly resembled the demonic entity within his sword. Hamza, running behind him, grabbed a troll by its neck and snapped it with little effort. The battle continued. Aliya in berserk mode showed no mercy to the hordes of orcs, trolls, dinosaurs, reptilians, and giants as he rampaged through the enemy lines. Though he was obliterating the enemy, the portals kept bringing in more, as if the gates to all the levels of hell had been opened. Demons of fire and imps began crawling in from out of the ground. Aliya kept swinging through them; his kills must have been in the thousands. Zulkirnaan, flaming hot, burned through the enemy with laser precision.

The enemy was many, and it had come to a point where they had begun to overpower our heroes. All hope seemed to be lost until, on the horizon, a flock of birds could be seen coming closer.

Wait! They were not birds, but wizards on their dragons. Jerreria had telepathically informed his friends to come and help once he knew that the Island of Dragons was under attack. They flew in and started to kill the evil army's giants, orcs, and other monsters and creatures. The battle was now favored on the side of light and not darkness. Only—where was the dragon scroll?

CHAPTER 23

Fight for the Fourth Scroll

Jerreria landed at Father Dragon's nest, at the highest altitude on the island. From that vantage point, a beautiful view of the pre-Jurassic land was observable. Many baby dragons took their first flights from the top; it was a test of initiation for the dragons in the wizard-carrying age. Jerreria remembered often sleeping at the top beside Father Dragon, for they shared a close bond. Jerreria's bloodline was of Abazel's. That was the sole reason why he had more of a connection to the dragons than the average wizard.

"Are you okay, Father Dragon?" he asked as he landed.

"No, Jerreria. I am near death. Usmak has slit me open and is retrieving the last scroll. It is in my heart. "Awhhhh!" he cried in agony. "I am the oldest dragon. The scroll kept me alive all this time. You have grown strong, like Abazel. Don't let us down." At that moment, Father Dragon died, and Usmak ripped through him, jumping out in front of Jerreria with one of the last two scrolls in his hand!

"Only a creature of reptilian bloodline can hold this scroll, Jerreria," Usmak said, slithering. Jerreria closed his eyes and yelled. Then he immediately began fighting Usmak. Usmak, also fast and agile, formed his Zusra swords. It was a battle to behold!

They looked like enchanted monks, fighting a battle of good versus evil…to the death. Jerreria sent a fist of wind at him then threw his electric spinning staff. Both were deflected by Usmak.

He then cloned himself, and all three began fighting one another. Jerreria landed an attack, and instantly Usmak turned to a hollow snake skin. He was a replica. The real one appeared out of the ground and hit Jerreria's clone, making it disappear. Usmak threw his sword at Jerreria, who blocked it with a light shield. They again started fighting each other, when Jerreria saw an opportunity and used his crystal staff to knock the scroll from Usmak's waistband into the air. Zulgini came sweeping in and swallowed it whole. Jerreria had telepathically told him to fly in just prior to that moment, knowing only reptilian blood—and dragon blood—could touch the scroll. If he had grabbed it himself, he would have immediately turned to star dust. What happened at that moment, no one would believe, unless they had been observing the spectacular transcendence themselves. Zulgini now had a chance against Serebus.

"Jerreria, what have you done!" Usmak hissed in anger, for he knew that he had let his master down.

"I am going to kill you, once and for all!" Isra said, appearing behind Jerreria and stabbing him through his back with his Zusra saber. His was different from Usmak's. It was made of dark blue-purple fire. In that very moment of weakness, Usmak also took advantage and sent his blood red Zusra cobra across the plain, straight into Jerreria's heart. "This is for Abubak!" Isra whispered in his ear as Jerreria fell to one knee.

Everything was getting blurry.

CHAPTER 24

The Evil Knight

Tachakra roared as he caught up to the orcs that held the princess captive. He had picked up her scent as they had passed him earlier on a nearby trail. He was watching them through the bushes when Naveen flew up. He looked at her momentarily then turned his gaze back to watching the orcs. They had stopped at a campsite guarded by two giants. Inside, hooded figures with blue demonic faces and arms with razor claws were chanting around a ceremonial black marble table, surrounded by large black Romanesque pillars. Tachakra, thinking this was his chance to save the princess before they took her in, lunged forward toward the orcs, claws out and mouth wide open. He fought them one by one, making his way up the ranks, tearing a chest open and ripping an arm off then, moving fast, clawing two to his right and left at once.

The giants saw him killing the orcs and came to their aid. Tachakra began fighting them, but our hero was no match for the giants, for he wasn't in his saber wolf form. He was kicked upward by one and smashed into the earth by another to the point where he was no longer visible. The orcs, caught briefly off guard, continued making their way up to the altar, as did the chanting, as the jinn began to form a smokeless blue fire around the table.

Aurora woke up and yelled in despair. Where was she? Why were they doing this to her? She had never seen such awful, evil-looking creatures. The jinn grabbed her and placed her on the altar as she screamed for someone to save her. At that moment, Aliya appeared in berserker mode on top of Hamza. He was enraged with anger and encased in a flame-like aura. There, he initiated his attack, killing everything in sight. Ripping Zulkirnaan through the giants, orcs, and jinn, every one of his moves was orchestrated like a master swordsman or Navy SEAL in our world. He sliced through flesh at lightning speed, gliding from one enemy to the next, showing none of them his back, but only his sword and red eyes before they were slaughtered.

"Call the dark knight!" the master jinn yelled, and from nowhere, a massive knight in black armor that covered everything except his face slammed down from the sky. It was Gadlin, and he was on top of Ragnor! Wait, they were both possessed with evil Zusra! What had Abubak done? He had turned our princess's guardian into a dark knight, a servant of their dark lord. Gadlin was wielding a sword, and it glowed in purple Zusra. Ragnor had also transformed and grown bigger. His fur was on fire with the same purple Zusra, also mixed with black. His eyes were also the same purple flame but with a black abyss for a center.

Aliya, in berserker mode, did not wait. He ran fearlessly at his enemy and was ready to kill. And why not? After all, he was a barbarian berserker. He smashed the knight off his old companion who now was infused with the evil force of the under realm. Hamza, protecting his new master, jumped at the possessed beast as they began to claw ferociously at each other.

Aliya's moves were no match for the knight though. The Zusra had taken over Gadlin and made him larger and stronger. They both moved with great speed and agility when attacking one another. Aliya did a forward slash as Gadlin stepped to the side and countered him. Aliya then swung Zulkirnaan first sideway then upward, but it was always out of reach of the dark knight, who then brought his sword down with incredible strength as a counterstrike after the prince's failed attempts. Aliya, unable to comprehend the knight's strength, was barely able to block his strike. One blow after another, the dark knight began overwhelming him. Aliya leaped in the air, performing a forward flip, his momentum swinging his sword. The dark knight grabbed his sword with one hand and threw him across the field. The knight now dashed forward and began a combo of slashes, each one heavily damaging the prince. His blood began to spill onto the ground from all his wounds. The dark knight delivered one final stab right through Aliya's abdomen, slowly inching it through until he pulled it out in one sudden motion. Aliya fell to the ground, now gasping for air.

The dark knight, satisfied with his kill, began to walk toward the sacrificial table when suddenly a faint tremor was felt in the land. Aliya's berserker mode wasn't enough, and his sword could sense he was losing his life energy. In an instant, his sword glowed...until it lit up with flames that began to engulf Aliya. The flame rose higher and higher, like a tornado spinning furiously into the sky. An image materialized within the fire. It was the Demon Kattz, whose soul was trapped in the sword. He was releasing his power to help the prince. Maybe he had become fond of him after being wielded by him for quite some time. Aliya rose up, his wounds healing from the mystical flame. There stood the prince, wielding Zulkirnaan, and Kattz, towering above him in the flame-engulfed tornado, holding a huge fiery version of the same sword. Together, they swung their swords downward, unleashing a fiery blast in one huge force that charged forward, cracking the earth toward the dark knight. Unable to move out of the way in time, his left arm was cut off, almost killing him altogether. Simultaneously, Hamza conquered Ragnor by grabbing his neck and sinking in his saber teeth.

Aliya ran toward the jinn that surrounded Aurora, and right before he was about to strike them, Isra appeared halfway out of a dark portal and grabbed our princess as she reached for the prince with her hands outstretched and her voice screaming, "Aliyaaa!"

Without warning, everything vanished like there had never been anything there except for Hamza, the prince, and the limb of the dark knight which had not teleported with Isra. Isra had taken Aurora into the Evil Forest to sacrifice her to the dark lord Dajjrah, enslave her soul, and use her as his queen to help him rule the universe.

CHAPTER 25

Aftermath

Zulgini transformed into a dragonoid. He was still a dragon, but his body had shrunk to fifteen feet in height, taking on a more human aspect. His arms and legs grew muscular and smaller. His tail was as long as his body, and his wings were now shrunken, but he could fly much faster than before. His white scales shined like pearls, and a type of mystical golden armor covered his body. Serebus shot its ice flame at him while he easily moved out of the way, rocketing toward him at full hypersonic speed. He flew 'till he was right behind the evil creature, and beginning at the tail, he plunged his claws into its flesh, right through its armor-like scales. He tore down the body at an extremely fast rate, heading toward the head. He vaulted over the back of Serebus's neck to directly in front of his face. With little effort, he stopped the dragon's movement with both hands and hit it with a laser beam released from his mouth, which was a concentrated form of his star flame, blending the different types of star fire together, as it ripped a hole into Serebus's head.

The lifeless beast began its descent downward through the sky, and at that instant, Zulgini felt Jerreria cry out in pain. He flew like lightning to help him, blasting Usmak with a white fireball from his hand as he sped toward the sorcerers in despair. Both magicians fearing for their lives, Isra and the snake king disappeared into separate portals. Jerreria's body fell, as if in slow motion, to the ground as Zulgini caught it before contact. How could he let his companion, his best friend, his master, get hurt? He knew only Elanor could help him. He flew off as fast as he could in search of her, our wizard's lifeless body in his arms.

On the other side of the island, Tachakra came out of the cracked earth to see Hamza, Aliya, and Naveen camping nearby. Aliya, now out of berserker mode, sat staring into the campfire. He had started a while ago at dusk and was trying to formulate a plan on how to save the princess but was only reminded of when she was being pulled through the portal by that horrendous being. Hamza, who lay a few feet from him, was also tired from the battling and limb-ripping he had done that day.

Our princess was being carried into a large lair within the Evil Forest as everyone, including Usmak and his reptile minions, the jinn, what was left of the dark knight, and the Zusra Ragnor bowed and pledged allegiance to their new queen-to-be.

Meanwhile, in the underwater kingdom Atlantia, Elanor listened to Zulgini who was now able to speak since he had absorbed the scroll.

"So only he can save him, if it's still possible?" the dragon asked aloud.

Elanor nodded as she had the body with the staff of Abazel placed in the eternal clamshell, within the blue aquatic water that Jerreria first used to communicate with Gora.

What felt like an eternity had passed, then a voice, from a faraway place, resounded: "Wake up, Jerreria. There is still much to be done!"

The End

ABOUT THE AUTHOR PAGE

Murtaza Syed was born in Tacoma, WA and moved at a young age living most of his life in San Jose, CA. In his adolescence, he excelled at writing literature and wanted to grow up to be like his mentor's J.K Rowling and J.R.R Tolkien.

One night he had a dream of a mysterious dimension and when he woke began writing the first chapter to his trilogy. He wants everyone to be able to escape to a mystical realm from their everyday lives and experience an adventure that will make all your problems go away, if even for a moment. Scrolls of Arcadia was written in the hardest of times as a guiding light, and he hopes it will illuminate his readers lives like it did his. Hang on to your wizard cap's because the adventure into Arcadia has just begun!

Made in the USA
Monee, IL
03 January 2023

20390960R00100